ABSOLUTE HARMONY

A HARMONY FALLS NOVELLA

ELIZABETH KELLY

EK PUBLISHING INC.

Edited by:
L. Nunn Editing

Cover art by:
EK Designs

ABSOLUTE HARMONY

Finding love after loss.

Widow Savina Ras is ready to love again.

Too bad Harmony Falls has a serious lack of older men interested in long-term commitment.

To make matters worse, she has an inappropriate crush on her late husband's best friend, vet tech Hal McGinnis. Hal is kind, sexy, and her closest friend.

At least, he used to be.

He's avoided her for a year, and Savina needs to move on. Then one unexpected, steamy encounter with Hal changes everything.

Hal's playing with fire and avoiding Savina in their small town proves nearly impossible.

But it's for the best.

Until Savina finds herself in a dicey situation, and Hal has to intervene. Their mutual attraction soon burns out of control, and once Hal has tasted Savina's sweetness on his lips, he can't walk away.

But for Hal, old guilt and regret are a heavy burden. Will their love be enough to bury that guilt for good?

Author's Note: "Absolute Harmony" is a novella in The Harmony Falls Series. It is a stand-alone story in the series.

———

CHAPTER 1

"Seriously, you're gorgeous. I've never seen an older woman as hot as you."

Savina gritted her teeth, keeping the smile she'd pasted onto her face cemented in place. "Thank you."

Her date sipped his drink before studying the packed pub. Savina drank the last of her wine and signaled the bartender for another. This would be her third glass, making it two more glasses than she usually drank, but she needed the liquid courage.

If you need liquid courage, you're making the wrong decision.

No, she wasn't. Michael was handsome and articulate, and he'd never once sent her a dick pic the entire time they'd texted. She was having sex with him tonight, and if she needed to be a little drunk to do it, that was okay.

"I'll be right back." Michael smiled at her. "Just need to use the restroom."

"Sure," she said.

She watched him weave past the tables, studying his

ass in his jeans. He had a nice butt. Of course, she'd known that from his Instagram posts. Michael loved posting gym selfies.

She, on the other hand, never set foot in the gym. In fact, if she was being truthful, she and Michael had very little in common.

What does it matter? Tonight is about hooking up, not finding your soulmate.

The bartender set a new wine glass in front of her and took her empty. She nodded in thanks before sipping at the wine. Tonight *was* about hooking up, and she would have a damn good time doing it. Michael was the perfect guy to break her dry spell.

He's younger than you!

That was true. Younger by a decade, in fact. But what did that matter? She'd been nearly fifteen years younger than Alan. She had zero interest in younger men, but after failing spectacularly with the men closer to her age, she'd decided to take a chance.

Michael slid back onto the barstool next to hers. She took another slug of wine when he rested his hand on her knee, hoping he hadn't noticed how she tensed.

"So," Michael's gaze dropped to her breasts and then back to her face, "you must get tons of compliments on how young you look, huh? Because you definitely don't look forty-three. I couldn't believe it when I read your bio on the dating app."

It was getting harder and harder to keep that smile on her face. She swallowed more wine and said, "I appreciate that, but I think I look my age."

"You don't. Trust me. I would normally never hook up with a woman older than me," Michael said, "but you can pass for in your thirties, so I told myself to go for it. Especially since the older ladies are well known to have high sex drives."

His lascivious grin made her smile slip. Did he think he was complimenting her?

Michael squeezed her knee before sliding his hand further up her thigh. She regretted wearing a dress when he slipped his fingers under the hem of it and - *sweet Jesus* - headed north.

She placed her hand on his, relieved when it stopped his forward motion. She glanced around the pub. No one paid attention to them, and she wasn't against PDAs, but was this a thing men did now? Just stuck their hand up a woman's dress in a crowded pub?

"What's wrong, gorgeous?" Michael squeezed her leg again.

"Nothing," she said and drained the rest of her wine. Her head buzzed, her pulse thumped, and she knew she was drunk. But that's what she wanted, right?

Sex for the first time since she'd gone from Savina Ras, wife, to Savina Ras, widow, required copious amounts of alcohol and a man she had no intention of ever seeing again.

"You ready to get out of here?" Michael waved down the bartender without waiting for her reply. "Hey, can we get our bill?"

The bartender brought their bill, and Michael scanned it as he pulled out his wallet. He handed his credit card to the bartender. "That's to cover my drinks."

Michael slid the bill across the bar to her. Her face burning, Savina took out some cash and handed it to the bartender. "Keep the change."

3

"Paying with cash, huh?" Michael said. "Old school, I dig it."

The bartender ran his card through the machine. Michael punched in some numbers and took the receipt, giving the bartender a defensive look when the man glanced at the receipt and then at him. "She covered the tip."

"Right," the bartender said. He looked to be in his late twenties or early thirties, with tattoos covering his arms and small spreaders in his earlobes. His dark hair was a little longer than she liked, but he had beautiful dark brown eyes and a lean and muscular body. If Savina had been twenty years younger, hell, even ten years younger, she might have considered hitting on him.

She'd been coming to the Thirsty Beaver Pub for years, but she'd never seen this guy before. A blessing, really. She had no desire for the usual bartenders, Rose or Colton, to see her on a date.

Not a date.

Right. Not a date.

She slid off the barstool and wobbled in her short, sensible heels.

"Whoa, you okay, gorgeous?" Michael slipped his arm around her, using her unsteadiness to get a good feel of side boob.

"Fine," she said, ignoring her urge to elbow him in the ribs but tugging away from his grip.

He held out his hand, and after a moment, she took it, allowing him to lead her out of the pub. The world was wavy on the edges, and she could feel the effects of the wine. She was sluggish and unsteady as she followed Michael to the parking lot.

"You okay to drive?" he asked.

"No," she said.

"No problem, we can take my car. You still in for fucking?"

She blinked at his forwardness, her brain trying to catch up with the rest of her. "Uh, yes, are you?"

"Oh hell, yeah." He stopped next to a green Nissan. "I told you before, you're fucking gorgeous. This is my car. Where do you live?"

"Oh, uh, I live outside of town," she said. "I thought we could go to your place?"

There was no way in hell she'd let a random hook-up come back to her house. Hell, she'd had second thoughts about even doing this with Michael since he lived right here in Harmony Falls, but he really had been the best of her matches. Besides, she was a grown woman. She could handle potentially running into a one-night stand in the grocery store.

But bringing Michael to the bedroom she'd shared with Alan was a big fat no. It didn't matter if the bed she slept on was new, and never once felt the weight of Alan's body. Didn't matter that she'd long since donated his clothes and most of his personal items. She still wouldn't let Michael within ten feet of the room.

"My roommates are home tonight," he said. "But if you don't care that they hear us fucking, then -"

"I'm good with a motel," she said quickly.

He frowned, "I don't want to pay for a motel. How far out of town do you live?"

"Too far," she lied.

He pulled her against him, grinning down at her. "Then I guess it's my place, and you'll have to keep the screaming to a minimum while I'm fucking you. Or," he reached down and squeezed her ass, "we can make sure that pretty mouth of yours is too busy sucking my dick to make noise."

Ugh.

"I'll pay for the motel," she said.

He shrugged, his hand still busy squeezing and cupping her ass. "Sure, whatever."

Without any warning, he dropped his mouth onto hers. She made a muffled squeak, her hands gripping his arms. Michael's mouth roamed over hers. He tasted like whiskey and, she grimaced inwardly, taco meat. His tongue invaded her mouth, too big and too wet, and her queasy stomach protested.

She'd kissed a few guys in the last year or so, and the kissing hadn't done a thing for her, which was a real head-scratcher because kissing was her *thing*. Nothing turned her on faster than kissing. Slow, deep, soft, demanding… it didn't matter. She loved to kiss.

Sure, but it's gotta be good kissing.

Her stomach lurched when Michael shoved his tongue so far into her mouth that she swore she could feel it touching her tonsils. She tried not to gag and failed, pushing away from Michael and staggering back. Luckily, Michael's car was behind her, or she would have fallen on her ass.

Michael frowned, his lips shiny and wet in the circle of light from the streetlamp above them. "What's wrong?"

Everything.

"Nothing," Savina said. "I … nothing's wrong."

He reached for her again, and when her stomach made another horrific lurch at the thought of Michael's lips plastered back onto hers, she pressed her hands against his chest and said, "I can't do this."

Michael scowled. "What do you mean you can't do this?"

"Is there another way to say it?" she asked.

A couple of women wearing microskirts and high heels walked by them, barely glancing at them as they headed toward the pub.

Michael flushed, his eyebrows drawing down even further and his lower lip pooching out like a little kid having a tantrum. "Are you fucking kidding me?"

"No, I'm not," she said. Michael's body blocked her sight line to the pub, but she could hear the soft swell of music and voices as the women opened the door. "I've changed my mind."

"You've changed your mind," Michael echoed. "Isn't that just fucking great? I could have gone out with a hundred women tonight who would have been happy to ride my dick, but I chose you. Because you're old and an easy lay, right? Or, at least, you're supposed to be."

"Fuck you," she said before shoving at his chest. "Get the fuck out of my way."

"What if I think you owe me?" Michael asked. "You've wasted a few hours of my time, so maybe I deserve something in return. Maybe you suck my dick right here in the parking lot like a good little cocksucker, and I won't -"

He made a pig-like squeal, and Savina gasped when Michael was spun around and shoved up against the silver SUV parked next to his car. His head banged against the window frame, and he bellowed a curse before glaring at the man standing before him. "What the fuck?"

"Hal?" Savina stepped toward the vet tech, but the world made a crazy slant, and - Christ - spun way faster than it should have been.

She slumped back against Michael's car, her pulse hammering erratically as she stared wide-eyed at Hal McGinnis - local vet tech, sexiest silver-haired fox in all of Harmony Falls, and her dead husband's best friend.

CHAPTER 2

Hal told himself it was none of his business when he saw Savina on her date. Told himself he didn't care as he watched her down three glasses of wine in rapid succession as that idiot beside her leered at her breasts and her hips.

Hell, he'd even convinced himself not to follow them out of the pub when Savina stood, and it was immediately clear she was drunk. She was a grown woman who knew how to handle herself and didn't need a babysitter.

He'd come to the Thirsty Beaver for a drink and to give him something else to do besides mope at home thinking about the one woman he could never have. That one woman being on a date at the pub only proved that God had a real fucked up sense of humour.

He'd only lasted a couple of minutes after Savina walked out the door before he gulped down the last of his beer, slapped some bills on the table, and headed out into the parking lot. He'd almost turned around and gone right back into the pub when he saw Savina and her date.

Hal might have been across the parking lot, but the light above them made it easy to see Savina's date had his tongue down her throat and his hands on her ass. He looked away as he wavered between going back into the pub and getting shitface drunk or climbing on his motorcycle and driving endlessly until the image of Savina being manhandled had left his brain. Maybe it would be gone by the time he hit Mexico.

He opened the pub door for two women in short skirts and high heels. They thanked him politely, their gaze sliding over him without seeing him. Not surprising. They looked to be in their twenties, and at fifty-two, he wasn't exactly in their age bracket, which was perfectly fine with him. He'd never understood why so many men his age dated women in their twenties. He'd never seen the appeal, and he never would.

He turned to follow them into the pub, glancing one last time over his shoulder at Savina. He froze, his guts tightening as he immediately went on high alert. He couldn't hear what her date said, but he'd known Savina for years. He recognized when she was upset, even just from her body language.

Hal jogged across the parking lot toward her, slowing down as he came up behind her date. His brain went to angry and protective caveman mode the minute he heard the asshole talk about Savina sucking his dick. He grabbed the guy, spun him around, and threw him up against a silver SUV.

The guy's head banged against the window frame, and he rattled off a curse before glaring at Hal. "What the fuck?"

"Hal?" Savina stared wide-eyed at him and pushed

away from the car she leaned against. She took a few staggering steps forward then fell back against the car with a soft groan.

"Who the fuck are you, asshole?" the guy snapped.

"Michael, he's a friend," Savina said. "He's -"

"Tell your fucking friend to keep his hands to himself," Michael snarled. "Unless he wants my fist buried in his face."

Hal barked laughter. "Go ahead and hit me, shithead."

"Hal," Savina said, "he's not worth it."

"Fuck you, bitch," Michael said and swung at Hal.

He dodged Michael's wild swing easily and then punched him in the stomach, pulling the punch at the last minute, so he didn't do serious damage to the loser.

Michael cried out, the colour fading from his face as he grabbed his stomach and bent over, coughing and gagging.

Hal watched silently, and when Savina staggered over to them, he stepped neatly in front of her, trying to ignore the feel of her soft weight as she crowded up against his back. "Hal, don't hurt him."

"Too late," Hal said. He knew Savina could hear the satisfaction in his voice, but fuck it. The guy shouldn't have spoken to her that way.

Savina pushed past him and touched Michael's shoulder. "Michael, are you -"

"Don't you fucking touch me," Michael snarled before coughing again. He straightened and one hand clasped across his stomach, glared at the both of them. "What the fuck, grandpa? You have to sucker punch me to win the fight?"

Hal rolled his eyes as Savina said, "That wasn't a sucker punch, you moron. You tried to hit him first."

"Whatever," Michael snapped. He staggered toward his car and flipped them both the bird before climbing in and driving away in a squeal of tires and spray of gravel.

Savina groaned and rubbed at her forehead. She swayed on her feet, and Hal took her upper arm. He could feel hard muscle beneath his grip - Savina was no delicate flower - but there was softness too. So much sweet softness. He looked her up and down. Instead of her usual jeans and shirt combo, she wore a light green dress that hugged her breasts and flared around her hips. Her dress ended just above her knee, and he stared at her bare calves. Her skin looked smooth and silky soft, and he wondered how it'd feel to have those legs hooked around his ass, her soft body cushioning his as he pounded into her over and over until he'd finally satisfied his endless ache for her.

His dick twitched in his pants, and guilt immediately rushed in. Lusting after his dead best friend's wife didn't exactly make him a real fucking Prince Charming, did it?

"Hal." Savina's voice sounded breathless and unsure. He was still staring at her tits like a pervert, and he forced his gaze to her face. For a moment, he thought he saw the same need, the same deep-seated desire reflected in her eyes and his cock hardened and pushed painfully against his jeans.

Savina looked away for a second, and when her pretty dark eyes returned to his, the desire, if it had ever really been there, was gone. He dropped his hand from her arm and smiled tersely at her. "You okay?"

"Fine," she said, then shook her head. "Scratch that. I'm tired and humiliated and drunk."

"You need to dump your boyfriend," he said.

She laughed, the sound bitter and jagged in the cool night air. "He's not my boyfriend. It was a first date."

"Don't see him again," he said.

"I'm not stupid," she snapped.

God, he fucking loved her temper.

She sighed and rubbed at her forehead again. "Sorry. Thank you for your help, Hal. I'll see you around."

"You can't drive home, Savina." He sounded angry. Hell, he was furious. What had she been thinking getting drunk on a first date with a guy she didn't know? It was reckless and stupid, and that wasn't Savina. She was the most level-headed and intelligent woman he knew.

"I'm aware of that," she said.

He tamped down his urge to lecture her. She didn't belong to him, and even if she did, it was patriarchal bullshit to think he could tell her what she could and couldn't do. But knowing that didn't help quell the anger inside of him. What would have happened if he hadn't been here? Savina was strong, but the guy had been bigger than her, and she'd had too much to drink. What if he'd forced Savina to -

Hal shut that thought down immediately. If he didn't, he would spend the rest of his life searching for that Michael fucker and beating the shit out of him when he found him.

His urge to lecture her, to scold her as if she were a child, reared its ugly head again. He swallowed it like bitter medicine and took Savina's arm when she started to walk away. "You've had too much to drink to drive."

"I know," she said, her temper lurking like a shadow in her words. "I'm calling an Uber."

"I'll drive you home," he said.

Happiness flickered across her face. "Did you ride your bike here?"

"Yes, but I don't have an extra helmet with me. I'll drive you home in your truck."

Her happiness faded like a dying star, and he hated that, but he wouldn't risk her safety. "Give me your keys."

She handed them over, and they walked silently to her truck. He wished she would weave again, or even stumble a little, any excuse to get his hands on her again. The guilt rolled in, relentless as the tide, and he wished, not for the first time, that he could shed its heavy weight. But that was nothing more than a pipe dream.

She climbed into the truck's passenger side, and he shut the door before sliding behind the wheel. Her vehicle started with a low rumble, and he drove out of the lot, the headlights cutting through the darkness.

He glanced over at her. She stared woodenly out the windshield. The darkness swallowed her expression, but it couldn't hide how tense she was. He sighed inwardly. They used to be friends. They used to talk and laugh and tease. Until he, or rather his fucking libido, had ruined it.

They'd spent countless evenings together in the first couple of years after Alan died, supporting each other through their mutual grief, and never once had he seen her as anything more than his best friend's wife. Did he notice how fucking beautiful she was? Yeah, of course, but no more than he noticed any other beautiful woman crossing his path. And in the first couple of years after Alan's death, Hal's grief and sense of loss had been too profound to think of Savina beyond Alan's grieving widow.

Until he didn't anymore.

His attraction to her had snuck up on him like a little

14

kid stealing from the cookie jar. One minute he was helping Savina build an Ikea dresser for the guest bedroom, and the next, he was wondering how she'd look on the bed, naked on her hands and knees and begging for his cock.

They were at the edge of town, and he followed the road to Savina's place. He knew the route as well as he knew the way to his place, his body on autopilot as he drove.

He could tell himself that his attraction had just suddenly appeared, but deep down, he knew the real truth. The last three months before that day had been a slowly boiling pot of noticing things he shouldn't have noticed. The silkiness of her soft brown hair, the perfect cupid's bow of her upper lip, the curve of her ass in her jeans. He'd buried those observations deep, pretending he didn't notice she was braless or the outline of her nipples against her thin shirt when he'd stopped by unexpectedly one day.

Until that fucking Sunday afternoon when he'd found himself in the guest bedroom, surrounded by Ikea parts, his cock a rigid pipe in his jeans, and a gently teasing Savina wanting to know why his face was suddenly so red.

He'd said nothing, just gave her a smile that was mostly a grimace because what could he say? I'm suddenly picturing you stuffed full of my cock, wasn't exactly an appropriate reply to give to your dead best friend's wife, was it?

That afternoon had been a turning point in their relationship. One Hal didn't want but couldn't stop. He'd begun to pull away, subtly and slowly, until here they were a year later, no longer friends and the tension so thick between them, he could taste it.

But what choice did he have? He was already suffocating in his guilt over Alan's death. The added guilt of lusting after Savina nearly cracked him in two.

He turned into Savina's driveway, parked the truck, and shut it off. Savina had left the front porch light on, providing just enough light to see her face. "Thank you for the ride home, Hal."

"You're welcome."

She hesitated, her fingers plucking at her dress hem. "Just leave my truck in the parking lot of the Beaver. I'll get Warren to give me a ride into town tomorrow to pick it up."

"I can leave it here and take an Uber back to the pub," he said.

She frowned. "No, absolutely not."

"You leave your truck at the Beaver overnight, and people will talk," he said.

She shrugged. "Like I care what they say."

He thought about arguing before letting it go. Changing Savina's mind was often like trying to keep sand off your feet at the beach. Impossible and pointless.

"Okay," he said. "You have a spare key for the truck, I assume?"

She nodded and studied him in the dim light. "Are you okay to drive? It's pretty late, and if you're too tired, you're welcome to sleep in the guest bedroom."

"No." He sounded angry, and he hated how Savina looked immediately guilty. But, holy fuck, she had no idea what that offer did to him. "I don't want to leave my bike in the parking lot overnight."

"Right," she said. "I wasn't thinking. Okay, well, thank you again."

She reached for the door handle, and desperate for even a few more minutes with her, he said, "How are Izzie and the puppies?"

Her smile, warm and genuine and so beautifully *her*, made every nerve in his body sizzle with awareness. "She's good. The babies are nursing well and gaining weight. Izzie is a wonderful mom to them."

"That's good," he said.

"You can come in and see them if you'd like."

"Another time," he said. "As you said, it's late."

She slid out of the truck, weaving a little as she grabbed the door. He clenched his hands around the steering wheel. "Do you need help getting into the house?"

He had no idea what the fuck he'd do if she said yes. He hadn't been alone with Savina in her house after darkness fell in nearly nine months. It was too... dangerous. Brought on too many fantasies and ideas that were best left buried.

"No," she said. "I'm fine. Goodnight, Hal."

"Goodnight, Savina."

CHAPTER 3

Savina parked her truck in the Brandt Veterinary Clinic's lot and cut the engine. She smoothed gloss onto her lips, pinched her cheeks, and studied herself in the rear-view mirror. She looked okay, maybe a little too excited for a woman taking her foster dog to an appointment to basically pee in a cup, but she couldn't help it. Hal worked as a vet tech at Brandt Clinic and she always looked this way whenever there was a possibility of seeing Hal. Which was pathetic and ridiculous, and it just seemed like such a fucking cliche to be lusting after your husband's best friend.

But she was, and she had long since stopped denying it.

It did make her a total asshole, though. Hal had been good to her and a solid rock for her to cling to after Alan's death. His wife had died seven years prior, and while the intensity of his grieving had lessened, he'd understood what Savina went through. He'd even been the one to tell her about the grief group for people who'd lost their partners. He no longer attended the group, but he was honest about how much it helped him the first few years and encouraged her to attend a meeting.

She'd gone with a fair amount of trepidation, but even after the first meeting, she knew it would help. She had her brother Warren and her niece Harper to help her through her grief, and although Warren knew too well what it felt like to lose a spouse, there was a specific understanding she received from other women who'd gone through the same loss.

Hal had been instrumental in helping her through the grieving process, and how did she repay his kindness? By lusting after him like a silly teenage girl. And now they were no longer friends, and the loss of Hal and his friendship was a brand new type of hell.

She'd had no guilt over Alan's death. Anger, sadness, despair… yes. But not guilt. After all, she hadn't given Alan stage four pancreatic cancer. But she had no one to blame but herself for what happened with Hal.

She slumped back in her seat, staring blankly at her truck's dashboard. It wasn't like she'd never noticed how handsome Hal was, even when she was married to Alan. But it was in more of a 'hey, that guy's good looking' way rather than an 'I want that guy to be balls-deep inside of me' way.

Until that damn Sunday afternoon. If she'd known asking Hal to help her build an Ikea dresser would have changed the course of their friendship, she'd have burned the fucking dresser. But how could she have known?

She hadn't expected that watching Hal sitting on the floor of her guest bedroom in a patch of sunlight, carefully and precisely sorting out screws, bolts, and pieces of wood would be the catalyst for bringing her lady bits back to life.

She'd chalked it up to a weird blip at first. Just her head, or rather her sex drive, getting confused for an afternoon. Could she blame it? She hadn't had sex in over two years, and Hal was kind, smart, and gorgeous. He'd been growing a beard – a new look for him - and while she'd teased him about the silver laced through it, she'd also secretly thought it made him look sexy as hell.

She'd pushed aside the tingling in her crotch and how her nipples had tightened when their hands touched while they built the dresser and told herself all afternoon that it meant nothing.

But she couldn't convince herself it was nothing when, later that night, as she masturbated alone in her bed, images of Hal kept popping into her head. The bulge of his biceps as he lifted the dresser and the hint of his flat stomach she'd seen when his shirt lifted. She'd rubbed her clit in hard, firm circles while she thought about her sudden desire to drop to her knees, unbuckle his belt, and find out just how big Hal's dick was.

That last image - her on her knees in front of Hal, his big hand palming the back of her skull as he urged her to suck his dick - had gotten her off like a fucking rocket. She'd ridden that orgasm high for nearly a minute, her body shuddering and shaking hard enough to make the bedsprings squeak.

She'd spent too much time over the last year wondering what Hal was like in bed. Would he be gentle or rough, tender or demanding? Her fantasies consumed her for the next few weeks after that Sunday afternoon. Hal bending her over the couch. Hal spreading her out on the big farm table in her kitchen and burying his face in her pussy like she was an all-you-could-eat buffet. Hal in her bed, his hands on her hips encouraging her to move harder and faster as she rode him to her release.

She'd tried hard to hide her newly discovered lust for him but failed spectacularly. Hal had started to pull away from her after that Sunday afternoon. Slowly at first and in subtle ways. Not replying to her texts as quickly as he used to, missing a few of their long-standing Sunday night dinners, and being too busy to go antiquing with her or catch the latest action movie at the theatre. She'd been so caught up in her lust for him that it had taken her a shamefully long time to notice the tension he now carried whenever he was near her.

Shame left her feeling sick and humiliated when it finally became apparent he was avoiding her. Her fawning over him, her obvious crush, had ruined their friendship, and she'd do anything to get it back.

But life didn't always work out the way one hoped or wanted. Even now, knowing Hal had ended their friendship because of her crush, she still wanted him. The few men she'd dated in the last nine months had all been a desperate attempt to forget how much she wanted Alan's best friend.

She smoothed a shaking hand over her face. She'd been sitting in the truck for nearly five minutes, and if she didn't get into the clinic in the next two, she'd be late for Izzie's appointment.

She turned in her seat to smile at the golden lab mix sitting patiently in the back seat. "You ready to be a good girl and pee on demand for us, Izzie?"

The dog's tail thumped on the seat.

"I'll take that as a yes," Savina said. "Also, can you send good vibes, that I don't see Hal this visit? I need more time to recover from the humiliation of the pub incident."

Izzie chuffed at her, and Savina smiled before climbing out of the truck. She opened the back door and took Izzie's leash. Izzie jumped down, sniffing at the ground. She started to squat, and Savina gave her leash a gentle tug. "Hey, not here, sweetie. Save that for the cup."

Izzie woofed but followed her toward the vet clinic's front door. The gravel crunched under their feet, and the air was crisp and clean after last night's crazy storm. Thankfully, the worst of the iciness on the roads had melted, and she'd had no issues driving to the clinic.

She stepped into the clinic. Until a few weeks ago, her brother Warren owned the vet practice, but he'd sold it to Nathan Henshaw, a young vet who started working at the clinic last year. Savina had questioned Warren's decision at first, but after meeting Nathan, any trepidation she felt disappeared. He was intelligent and kind and had a great deal of respect for Warren, and while it was a bit of a rough patch for him right now in terms of the townfolk accepting him as the new owner, she hoped it would blow over quickly.

For the first time in a long time, her brother seemed happy and relaxed, and she wanted it to stay that way. He, more than anyone, deserved peace.

"Hi, Savina!" Fatima, one of the receptionists, waved at her from the desk. "You're here for your appointment with Izzie?"

"That's right," Savina said.

"Great, let's get you into the room. Dr. Warren will be right with you."

She and Izzie followed Fatima into the room. After a quick pat to Izzie, Fatima left. Not two minutes later, the door opened, and Warren stepped inside. "Hey, Savina."

"Hey. How are you?" she asked.

"Good. That was some storm last night, huh? Any troubles driving in?" Warren petted Izzie.

"No, the roads were fine. Thanks again for taking me to pick up my truck yesterday morning."

He grinned and leaned against the counter that housed a sink and a small weight scale. "You're welcome. Anyone say anything to you yet about your truck being at the Beaver all night?"

"No, but I haven't been to town since I picked it up. Why, have you heard anything?"

His grin widened, and she rolled her eyes. "Small town gossip is the worst. Let me guess, you've heard I'm having drinking problems."

Warren laughed. "That about sums it up, which is hilarious because I can't remember the last time I saw you drink more than a single glass of wine. Why did you drink so much Thursday night anyway?"

Well, at least that quelled one fear. Hal hadn't said anything to Warren about what he saw Thursday night.

"I had a date, and it went horribly," she said.

A frown crossed her brother's face. He was older than her by a decade, she'd been an oops baby, and he'd spent most of his life acting like a second dad to her. "What happened?"

"Nothing to worry about," she said. "I handled it."

No, Hal handled it.

She ignored her inner voice as Warren said, "All right. Well, be careful out there."

"You be careful too," she said.

His cheeks reddened. "What do you mean?"

"I saw your profile on the dating app, buddy," she said. "The one for people over forty."

His cheeks were now a flaming red, and she had to hold in the giggles as he said, "Shit. Are you on that app too?"

"Yes," she said. "I'm glad you're dating. Have you told Harper yet?"

"Sort of. She's supportive of her old man dating."

"Good," Savina said.

"So, what's going on with Izzie?" He crouched and rubbed Izzie's head before reaching under her and palpating her belly as he studied her milk-filled nipples. "No signs of mastitis."

"No, but I think she might have a UTI. She's peed twice in the house since yesterday morning, and that's not like her. Especially since she has access to the fenced-in yard through the doggie door," Savina said.

"Okay, we'll get a urine sample and test it," Warren said. "I'll take her to the back and ask Hal to -"

The knock made them both turn as Fatima stuck her head into the room. "Dr. Warren? The radiologist from Dynamic Labs is on line one. I know you've been waiting all morning to talk to him."

Warren stood. "Savina, do you mind?"

"No," she said.

"Great. I won't be long. Actually, why don't you take Izzie to the back and let Hal know we need a sample."

Her stomach dropped, her hope that she might avoid Hal crashing like waves on a beach, but she nodded. "Sure, that's no problem."

CHAPTER 4

Holding Izzie's leash, Savina followed Warren through the lobby and past the swinging door that led to the back. Warren headed to his office, and her nerves singing high soprano, she ventured further into the back. She found Hal in the cat room and smiled tentatively at him. "Hello, Hal."

He set the big black cat he held in one of the smaller kennels and latched it. "Hi, Savina."

"How are you?" she asked.

"Good. How can I help you?"

He was all brisk business and no-nonsense profesionalism.

"Izzie might have a UTI. Warren is on a phone call, but he asked me to bring her back to get a urine sample."

"Okay."

She moved back, trying not to gasp when Hal walked past her, and his bare arm brushed against hers.

Oh, good, new masturbating material.

Her face flushed, and she wasn't sure if it was from

Hal's touch or the embarrassment that a brief brush of his skin against hers was all it took to turn her on.

Probably a little of both.

Hal grabbed a clear container, and she and Izzie followed him down the narrow hallway that led to the side exit. The yard was fenced in, and she dropped Izzie's leash to allow her to wander.

Hal gave Izzie a pat when she walked over to him. He followed her around patiently, the container in hand, as Izzie sniffed and snorted her way across the lawn.

"Go pee, Izzie," Savina said. "Go pee, good girl."

Izzie's tail wagged at the sound of her voice, but she continued her investigation of the lawn. Five minutes later, Izzie had sniffed what Savina assumed was every blade of grass in the yard but hadn't peed.

"Sorry," she said to Hal, feeling embarrassed for some reason. "I don't know why she won't pee."

Hal picked up Izzie's leash and rubbed her head when she sat at his feet and leaned against him. "Just being stubborn, I guess."

"Yeah." The cold air gave Savina goosebumps, and she rubbed her arms briskly.

"Instead of waiting in the cold, I'll give you a container, and you can get a sample at home to bring into the clinic," Hal said.

"Okay." She couldn't fool herself into thinking Hal wasn't trying to limit his time with her. She could practically smell his discomfort.

You need to apologize, Savina.

She did and now seemed as good of a time as any. Better to get it over with, right?

"I want to apologize for Thursday night," she said.

He continued to pet Izzie's head without looking at her. "You weren't the one acting like an asshole."

"No, but I'm sorry that you got dragged into that mess. My dating life shouldn't be affecting you."

His whole body was now weirdly tense, and she took a few steps toward him and Izzie. "Hal, are you okay?"

He raised his head, and she caught her breath at the anger on his face. Why would apologizing make him angry?

"You need to be more careful, Savina," he said.

"Excuse me?"

"With who you date," he said, "and how you behave around them."

"What is that supposed to mean?" Anger immediately curled at her edges, sharp and painful.

"It means getting drunk on a first date with a guy you barely know was dumb." Hal dropped Izzie's leash, and she wandered away to sniff at the grass again. "I know you're not stupid, Savina, so what the hell were you thinking, getting drunk?"

Disbelief mixed with her anger. "Since when did you get so judgmental, Hal?"

"I'm not being judgmental. I'm looking out for a friend," he snapped.

"Friend? Oh, now, we're friends? You've been avoiding me for nearly a year, or have you forgotten that?" she said. "That isn't something a friend does."

"It doesn't change the fact that you put yourself in real danger that night," he said. "If I hadn't been there -"

"If you hadn't been there, I would have taken care of the problem myself. I'm not some helpless little girl."

"Drinking too much made you vulnerable." Hal's face

was red, and his usual calm and easygoing nature had vanished. "Why would you be so reckless?"

"It's none of your business," she said. "Izzie, come."

"I deserve an explanation," Hal said.

"Like hell you do," she said.

His eyebrows drew down in a fierce scowl. "Drinking that much was stupid and -"

Her temper, which she'd been clinging to by the thinnest of rope, snapped like a dead branch. "I needed to be drunk to fuck him, okay?"

Hal stared at her like she'd grown a second head. "You were going to have sex with that guy?"

"Yes, I was." She stared defiantly at him. "Do you have a problem with that?"

"I have a problem with you needing to be drunk to sleep with some guy," Hal snarled.

"Well, excuse me for needing a little liquid courage to have sex for the first time in over three years," she said.

"If you need to be drunk, then you're not ready," he said.

"Don't," she said. "You don't get to tell me what I am or am not ready for. Fuck right off with that bullshit, Hal."

"I'm trying to keep you safe," he said.

"No, you're just pissed that your best friend's wife is moving on with her life. Alan's gone, Hal, and it isn't fair of you to think I should stay celibate for the rest of my life."

It was the wrong thing to say. Her eyes widened when Hal stalked toward her. She backed up until her back hit the clinic wall, the coldness from the brick seeping through her clothing as Hal braced his hands on the wall and penned her in.

"That is not what this is about," he said in a dangerously quiet voice. "This is about me keeping you safe."

"That isn't your job," she said. "You thinking you have the right to tell me what to do is rich, considering that you barely speak to me anymore. In fact, I... Hal? Are you even listening to me?"

Hal was staring at her mouth, and her breath released in a squeaky sigh when his gaze dipped to her breasts. "Hal?"

He slowly lifted his gaze to her, and every muscle in her lower stomach clenched tight at the look on his face. He wanted her. It had been a long time since a man had looked at her like Hal was, but she recognized desire when she saw it. Her nipples pebbled tight, and her pussy throbbed with a need to be filled.

Images flooded her head. Images of Hal pulling down her jeans and panties. Hal freeing his cock, pushing her thighs apart, and fucking her right there against the clinic wall. Fucking her until that empty ache was gone, until nothing mattered but the feel of his cock, the sound of his voice, the glorious chase for her orgasm.

"Savina," Hal's voice was low and tortured. "Christ, whatever you're thinking... stop."

"Hal," she whispered before raising one shaky hand and pressing it against his chest. "Hal, I need... please."

He groaned and stepped forward, bridging the tiny gap between them, and pressed his mouth against hers. Savina fisted his shirt, pulling him even closer as she returned his kiss. His lips were warm and firm, and she shuddered with pleasure when he flicked his tongue against the seam of her lips. She opened for him, welcoming his tongue with soft moans and gentle licks.

He explored her mouth with a slow, almost lazy style that made desire drip through her like sweet honey. This was what she craved, what she needed. She didn't care that her toes were going numb from the cold or that Hal was supposed to be working. She could kiss Hal forever and never get tired of it.

Hal's knee nudged at hers, and she spread her legs, moaning into his mouth when his thick thigh pressed up against her pussy. She ground herself shamelessly against his leg, needing friction and relief for that endless ache.

She reached for his belt buckle, whining in frustration when Hal grabbed her hands and lifted them over her head. He pinned her arms to the wall with one hand around her wrists, and she arched against him when he nipped at her throat.

"I want to touch you," she said.

He shook his head, his hands tightening around her wrists. "No."

"Why not?" She really should have been more embarrassed than she was by how needy she sounded.

He kissed his way to her ear, sucking lightly on her earlobe as his other hand rested on her ribcage just below her breasts. "Because I'll fuck you right here if you put your hands anywhere near my dick, sweet Savina."

She moaned, grinding her pussy against his thigh again. "I'm good with that."

He grunted in surprise before staring at her. His nostrils flared as he sucked in a harsh breath. "Fuck, you're being serious."

She rubbed against his thigh again, biting at her bottom lip when his thumb rubbed along the underside of one breast. "Hal, I -"

"Hey, Hal? Do you have time to -"

Nathan's voice dropped off in a surprised grunt. Hal stared at the young veterinarian who'd stepped out from the side door, his hands tightening almost painfully around Savina's wrists before he let her go and stepped back.

Embarrassment flooding through her, Savina hurried toward the door. "Izzie, come."

Her voice was high-pitched and weird sounding, and she could have hugged the lab mix with gratitude when the dog immediately followed her into the clinic.

She grabbed Izzie's leash and, keeping her head down and praying she didn't run into Warren, walked past the swinging door and into the clinic foyer. Thankfully, Fatima was on the phone, and Savina waved briefly at her before escaping.

She lifted Izzie into the truck, climbed in behind her, and slammed the door shut. She stared at herself in the rearview mirror. Her lip gloss was smeared, her cheeks were bright pink, and her eyes were wild.

"Oh God," she groaned before staring at Izzie. "What did I just do?"

Izzie chuffed, and Savina buried her face in her hands for a few seconds before starting the truck. "This is bad, Izzie. This is 'I have to move to a new town' bad."

Izzie laid down on the seat, unconcerned with Savina's plight. Her heart still a frantic beat against her ribcage, Savina drove toward home.

CHAPTER 5

"You ready to tell me what's wrong yet?"

Hal ran the brush down Molly's side again. Molly turned her big head to investigate Hal's shirt pocket for a piece of carrot, and Hal rubbed the horse's forehead. "Why do you think something's wrong?"

"Whenever you're upset, I find you in my stables brushing the horses." Solomon leaned against the wall. "Not that I mind the free labour, but you'll feel better if you tell me what's wrong instead of bottling it up."

Hal studied the big man. Solomon Whitaker owned Whitaker Ranch, one of the largest and most prosperous ranches in Harmony Falls. As teenagers, Hal, Solomon, and Alan had been inseparable. And while they'd taken very different career paths, they'd remained best friends, supporting each other through the best and worst parts of their lives for the last forty years.

Hal ran the brush across Molly's back. "I kissed Savina last weekend."

There was no judgment on Solomon's face which Hal

appreciated, but he still felt defensive. "I know, I'm an asshole."

"Oh, yeah, you're an asshole, but not for kissing Savina," Solomon said with a slight grin. "Come on, let's go to the house and get a drink before you brush Molly raw."

A few minutes later, they were sitting in the comfortable leather chairs in Solomon's study. Solomon poured them each a glass of whiskey, and Hal sipped at the amber liquid, relishing the burn in his belly. The study door opened, and Solomon's wife, Heather, stuck her head into the room. "Hey, Hal."

"Hi Heather, how are you?"

"Good, thanks." She smiled at him before turning to Solomon. "I'm leaving for town. Do you need anything?"

"I'm good. Drive safe, sweetheart."

She blew him a kiss and left, shutting the door behind her.

After a few minutes of silence, Hal said, "Say something, for God's sake."

"I'm just trying to figure out when you had the opportunity to kiss Savina Ras. You've become a ghost when it comes to her."

"She was at the clinic with her foster dog."

Solomon grinned. "Shit, man, you kissed her while you were working?"

Hal sipped more whiskey. "Yes. And Nathan caught us."

"You still got a job?" Solomon asked in his usual blunt way.

"Yes. Nathan was surprisingly understanding," Hal said.

"Savina kiss you back or slap your face?" Solomon asked.

Hal stared at him, and Solomon shrugged. "Savina's always had a bit of a temper."

"She kissed me back," Hal said.

"So, why do you look like you did when we got caught siphoning gas from Coach Vernon's car back in grade twelve?"

"Why the fuck do you think? I kissed my best friend's wife," Hal said.

"No, you kissed your best friend's widow. And it ain't like Alan's gonna rise out of the grave to give you shit over it."

At Hal's glare, Solomon shrugged again. "I miss him as much as you do. Doesn't mean what I say isn't true. Alan's not coming back, and neither is Mary. Why shouldn't you and Savina find happiness together?"

"Because it's...." Hal swallowed down the rest of that sentence. Telling Solomon about his guilt over Alan's death would only lead to questions. Questions Hal didn't want to answer. If Solomon knew about Hal's pettiness and jealousy over losing his wife while Alan and Solomon still had theirs, he'd never speak to Hal again. It would be the final blow to completely shatter Hal's bruised and cracked heart.

"Because it's what?" Solomon asked.

"Wrong," Hal said.

"It's not cheating," Solomon said.

"I know that. But it's still wrong."

When Solomon got that familiar 'you're wrong and here are all the reasons why you're wrong' look on his face, Hal said, "It feels wrong to *me*, Solomon."

"Okay," Solomon said. "So, have you and Savina talked about what happened?"

"No," Hal said, "and I don't plan on talking to her about it. It was a one-off thing, a mistake that will never happen again."

"You sure about that?" Solomon asked.

"What's that supposed to mean?" Hal said.

"It means I saw how you looked at Savina before you started avoiding her."

"I'm not avoiding her," Hal said. "We were just never that close. It was Alan who connected us, and with him gone...."

"Well, ain't that a load of horse shit," Solomon said. "You and Savina were thick as thieves after Alan died. Savina's told Heather more than once that you helped her get through the worst of the grief."

Hal stared moodily into his whiskey. "I helped her because I knew what she was going through and because a few weeks before he died, Alan asked me to be there for her."

"But only for the first two years after his death?" Solomon said. "After that, she was on her own, is that it?"

"I can't be around her!" Hal snapped. "Not when all I can think about it is being in her goddamn bed, kissing her, touching her and...."

He drank the rest of his whiskey in one large gulp before standing and stalking to the bookshelf. He stared blindly at the books. He hadn't meant to say that, but Solomon had a way of getting confessions from people.

Solomon's hand landed on his shoulder and squeezed. "There's no guilt in being attracted to Savina. She's a beautiful, kind, and generous woman."

"She deserves better than me," Hal said. "She deserves… Alan."

"Alan was a good man," Solomon said. "But so are you, and if there's something between you and Savina, that's worth exploring. Both of you know more than most how short life is."

"I can't," Hal said hoarsely. "I won't take advantage of Savina's loss just to get into her bed."

"It's not taking advantage of her if she wants you as well."

"She's still grieving. She doesn't know what she wants," Hal said.

"Jesus Christ." Exasperation and love mixed in Solomon's tone. "Are you listening to yourself? Since when did Savina not know her own mind? It's been three years since Alan died, and she's a damn good looking woman. She'd have no shortage of guys hitting on her, and she's probably fucked some of them."

"She hasn't," Hal said. "She told me she hasn't slept with anyone since Alan died."

Solomon raised an eyebrow at him. "That's pretty intimate shit for her to be sharing with you, especially since you've been ghosting her for the last year."

"I saw her on a date with some punk asshole at The Thirsty Beaver. He said some rude shit to her in the parking lot, and I…."

"Beat the shit out of him?" Solomon said with a grin.

"He tried to hit me," Hal said.

Solomon bellowed laughter, and, his face red, Hal said, "I only punched him once, and it was in self-defense."

Solomon laughed again. "I'm sure Savina was appreciative."

"At the time, yes. Later, not so much."

Solomon stared questioningly at him, and Hal said, "I might have tried to lecture her at the vet clinic about how she couldn't drink while she was on a date, especially when it was with a guy she knew nothing about."

"Christ," Solomon said. "So, she kissed you instead of ripping your nuts off and stuffing them up your own ass, huh? Savina's getting soft."

"She was pissed, and rightly so. I was being a total dickhead. But she also told me she was drinking because it was the only way she could have sex with the guy. I told her if she had to get drunk to fuck him, then she wasn't ready for sex."

"Or, she's ready and just needs someone she trusts for her first time back in the saddle, so to speak," Solomon said.

Hal studied him, and Solomon said. "Think about the first time you had sex with a woman after Mary died. It'd been, what, five years? But I bet it was still weird and awkward, and you felt guilty, right?"

Hal nodded. "Yeah."

"If I remember correctly, it was a random woman you met at a bar in Willington?"

"Yes," Hal said.

"I bet you even had a couple of drinks beforehand to help with the nerves and the guilt," Solomon said.

"I did." Hal groaned. "Christ, now I'm a hypocritical asshole."

"Yup," Solomon said.

"Don't soften the blow or anything," Hal said.

Solomon grinned before squeezing his shoulder again. "You care about Savina and want her to stay safe. I get it.

And for the record, I think you should volunteer to be the first guy she sleeps with. She trusts you, and I doubt she'd need to be drunk to do it."

"Sleeping together would destroy our friendship," Hal said.

"It's already ruined," Solomon said. "I know you don't want to hear that, but it's the truth."

"I can't sleep with her," Hal said.

"Then you have to let her live her life too. You need to let her make her own mistakes and figure her shit out. Which includes fucking guys she shouldn't."

"I know," Hal said. "It's just easier said than done."

"Ain't that the fucking truth." Solomon clapped him on the back. "Come on, we'll have another whiskey, and I'll show you the new horse Wyatt's breaking in. He's giving Wyatt a real run for his money. And you're staying for Sunday dinner, no fucking arguing."

CHAPTER 6

"I'm so sorry I'm late, Wanda." Savina sank into the chair across from Wanda. "I volunteered at the library, and story time ran late."

"Don't worry about it, sweetheart." Wanda pushed a coffee across the table. "I got you your usual."

"You're a lifesaver." Savina sipped at the hot liquid. Grind my Beans was busy this afternoon, as it usually was on a Sunday afternoon. She glanced around the store for her niece Harper, who'd been working at the coffee shop since she returned from New York.

"If you're looking for Harper, you just missed her," Wanda said. "She was finished her shift. She said to tell you hello, but I'll be honest – she didn't look her usual happy self."

Savina sighed. "She's having a tough time right now."

"Does it have something to do with the new vet, Nathan Henshaw?"

"What have you heard?" Savina said guardedly.

"Just that they might be an item. Seo-Jun hasn't been

quiet about sharing that Nathan was waiting for Harper here at the coffee shop a couple of weeks ago," Wanda said.

"They were growing close," Savina said, "but they decided to end it last Wednesday. Harper stopped by the house this morning for coffee and to talk. She talked to her dad last night and realized that ending things with Nathan was a mistake. Nathan is out of town, but when he returns on Tuesday, she plans to talk to him. She's worried about how it will go, though."

Usually, Savina wouldn't tell anyone about Harper's business, but Wanda was a dispatcher for the sheriff's office. The only person more closemouthed about people's business than Wanda was the actual sheriff, Gideon Walker.

Wanda nodded sympathetically. "Love is always a blessing, but it can rattle a person up something fierce when it wants to."

"Isn't that the truth," Savina said. "Did you go to the meeting this week?"

Although Savina had known Wanda enough to smile and nod to her on the street, it wasn't until the last three months that she'd gotten to know the tall and elegant looking Black woman better. Wanda's husband Murray had died in July, and Wanda had started attending the group for grieving spouses. Savina still attended the group once or twice a month, and while it was the shittiest of ways to make a new friend, Savina felt a real connection with Wanda and valued her friendship.

"I did," Wanda said. "It was a good meeting, lots of crying, but for the first time, I wasn't the one sobbing into my coffee cup."

Savina reached out and took Wanda's hand. "Grief comes in waves."

"It does," Wanda said. "I'm thankful this week has been better than the last few."

"Good." Savina squeezed her hand. "One day at a time, right?"

"That's right. So, how did it go?"

Savina blinked at her. "How did what go?"

Wanda laughed. "If you've already forgotten your date, it couldn't have gone well."

"It wasn't what I'd hoped," Savina said. "It ended with Hal McGinnis punching him in the Thirsty Beaver's parking lot."

Wanda's dark brown eyes went round. "Goodness. I'm gonna need all the details."

Savina laughed and did a quick retelling of the story. Wanda sat back in her seat when it was finished, her long fingers toying with her coffee cup lid. "Well, that was quite heroic of Hal."

"It was," Savina said shortly. "Anyway, it's back to the drawing board, or dating app as the case may be, to try again."

"Right." Wanda gave her a look that made Savina squirm in her seat.

"What?" she asked.

"What aren't you telling me?" Wanda asked.

"Nothing," Savina said.

Wanda smiled. "I know we've only been friends for three months, but it feels longer, doesn't it? Like we've been friends for years."

"Yes," Savina said.

"That's probably why I can tell when you're not telling me something," Wanda said with another smile.

"Dammit," Savina sighed. "Stop reading me so well, Wanda."

"Can't help it," she said. "Now, spill."

Savina hesitated before deciding to be honest. "Hal has been Alan's best friend since they were teenagers. After Alan died, Hal was my rock. We were friends before Alan died, and we became, well, best friends after. Then one day last year, I started noticing how amazing his ass is and wondering what he would be like in bed, and I did a piss poor job of hiding it. Hal realized what was happening and … well, he drifted away, you know? We used to spend hours together, and now I'm lucky if I even run into him on the street. He's avoided me for the last year, and it's embarrassing as hell, and I miss him. The loss of his friendship is like another piece of my old life with Alan was torn away."

"I'm sorry, sweetheart," Wanda said.

"You haven't heard the worst of it yet," Savina said. "Hal and I fought at the clinic last Saturday about what happened on my date, and it ended with us kissing."

"Wow." Wanda sat up straight. "That's… unexpected."

"Tell me about it. Apparently, Hal is attracted to me too, and now I'm unsure what to do. Nathan caught us, which was beyond humiliating, and I took off like a coward. I called Hal the next day to apologize, but he didn't answer the phone. I finally texted him, and I know he read it, but he hasn't replied. He's avoiding me again."

She sipped at her coffee. "I'm so confused and don't know what to do. I mean, do I force Hal to talk about what happened between us, to acknowledge that there's something between us, or do I leave it be? The guilt on his face after we kissed… it made me feel terrible, Wanda. I can only imagine how awful he felt."

"Maybe the guilt was more about… how can I put this… doing non-work related things while at work," Wanda said.

"Maybe," Savina said. "Which also makes me feel like a real jackass, and I don't even know how much trouble he got into with Nathan because it's not like I can casually ask Warren if Hal was disciplined at work."

"Maybe you could stop by his place," Wanda suggested.

"Honestly, I doubt he'd even answer the door," Savina said. "I wish he would acknowledge the attraction between us. Maybe then I wouldn't feel so foolish or so guilty. And I think if we slept together, even once, it would help to…."

She stopped, rubbing her hand across her forehead. "Shit. I'm sorry, Wanda."

"For what?" Wanda asked.

"Listening to me go on and on about my desire to bone Hal McGinnis isn't what you need to hear right now. I'm being incredibly insensitive."

Wanda shook her hand, reaching out to retake Savina's hand. "No, you're not. You're a wonderful person who is going through some shit and needs to talk to a friend about it. I'm happy to be that friend, sweetheart."

"Are you sure?" Savina asked. "I can't help but think how I would have been at this stage of grief, and I'm not sure I'd be up to listening to my whining."

"Yes, but you're not me," Wanda said. "I find it oddly helpful. You've gone through this horrible journey before me, and seeing you now gives me hope. Hope that eventually, this stupid all-consuming grief will diminish and that, with time, I might find myself willing to go on dates and take a chance on love again."

She made a face. "Now I sound like the selfish one. I hate that you're struggling with your feelings for Hal."

"It's not feelings," Savina said. "It's just an attraction. One that could be cleared up with a night of sex."

"Right," Wanda said.

"It is," Savina insisted. "I'm positive that if Hal and I have sex, we could return to being friends and how things used to be between us."

Wanda grinned. "Has that plan worked out for anyone in the history of ever?"

"So, you don't think I should sleep with Hal?" Savina asked.

"Oh, I think you should bang him like a screen door. That boy is fine as hell," Wanda said. "But I'm not certain it'll fix your friendship how you want it fixed."

"It doesn't matter, anyway," Savina said. "Hal's made it clear that the kiss was a mistake, and he wants to continue avoiding me. I need to move on."

"Okay," Wanda said. "So, are you going to try the app again?"

"Yes," Savina said. "In fact, I have a date on Friday with a very nice man named Scott. He's my age and manages the garden center at Home Depot. He loves animals, gardening, and spending time with family."

"Sounds like he has potential," Wanda said.

"I hope so," Savina said.

"Text me and let me know how the first date goes," Wanda said.

"I will."

"Perfect. Now," Wanda took out her phone and scrolled through it, "take a look at this picture and be an excellent friend who tells me these are the perfect pair of shoes, and I'd be a fool not to buy them."

Savina laughed and took the phone. "Yes, ma'am."

CHAPTER 7

"I think you'll really love this place." Scott held out her chair for her, and Savina smiled at him as she sat down.

"Thank you. I remember hearing good things when the Bronze Blossom opened last year, but I haven't had the chance to try it yet."

"They make a great carbonara dish." Scott was staring around the restaurant, and he seemed jittery and nervous.

"Is everything okay?" Savina asked.

"Yep, just great." Scott's smile struck her as false, but she returned his smile before studying the mid-sized restaurant. It was about half-full, and she liked the casual atmosphere and the blue monochromatic colour scheme.

A blonde woman with badly drawn eyebrows and lips painted a frosted pink stopped at their table. She wore the servers' black pants and white shirt uniform and plunked two menus on the table.

"Welcome to Bronze Blossom. Our special tonight is...."

The server trailed to a stop, her entire body stiffening as she stared at Scott. Anger crossed her face, and Savina blinked in surprise when the woman turned a smoking hot look of hatred her way.

Her nostrils flaring, she said, "My name is Tabitha. I'll be your server tonight."

"Hello, Tabitha," Scott said, his voice squeaking a little when he said her name. "I'm Scott, and this beautiful woman is my date Savina. She's forty-three but looks thirty-three, don't you agree? I've never seen a woman this gorgeous in my life."

"Uh, hello," Savina said, alarm bells clanging to life in her head.

"Nice to meetcha'." If Tabitha could set her on fire with her gaze alone, Savina would be in dire need of a fire extinguisher.

"I'll have a beer, whatever's on tap, and what would you like to drink, gorgeous?" Scott gave her a broad smile, but a weird light shone in his gaze and his fingers tapped out a staccato beat on the table.

"A glass of your house wine, please," Savina said.

"Coming right up," Tabitha said.

She turned and started to walk away, stopping and giving Scott a falsely sweet smile when he grunted out a curse. "That was my foot you just stomped on."

"Oh, I'm so sorry, sir. I'll be sure to be more careful in the future." Tabitha stalked away.

Scott gave Savina another nervous smile before flipping open his menu. "Would you like to share an appetizer?"

"Sure," Savina said.

She opened her menu, her stomach dropping when

Scott said, "Hal! Hey, good to see you, man."

This cannot be happening.

Plastering a smile on her face, Savina looked up. Hal, looking as shocked to see her as she was to see him, slowed to a stop next to their table.

Scott stood and shook Hal's hand. "How are you?"

"Good, thanks," Hal said. He wore jeans and a long sleeve shirt that clung to his upper body, highlighting the bulge of his biceps and the broadness of his chest. Christ, she would start drooling any minute.

He glanced at Savina. "Hello, Savina."

"Hi, Hal," she said.

"Oh, you two know each other," Scott said. "Small towns, am I right?"

Hal smiled stiffly. "Yeah."

"How do you know Hal?" Savina asked.

"We're on the same team in the over forty baseball league," Scott said.

There was an awkward silence before Hal said, "I'll let you get back to your dinner."

He walked away, heading to a table on the far side of the restaurant. He sat down just as his server arrived with his food. She was pretty with long dark hair and a curvy figure, and when she smiled at Hal, and he returned her smile, jealousy clawed at Savina's insides.

She looked back at her menu, her face hot, and tried to concentrate on her date. Other than the initial weirdness with their server, Scott seemed nice. He was good looking, and they were hitting it off so far. She would have a couple of glasses of wine, enjoy some good conversation, and then take Scott home and fuck him. Easy as pie.

"SO, I TOLD MY EMPLOYEE THAT IF HE DIDN'T REMEMBER to water the petunias daily, I'd have no choice but to dock his pay for every tray that died. I mean, it's not rocket science, right? You work in a garden center. You're required to water flowers." Scott rolled his eyes.

Savina smiled at him and wondered if it was possible for a brain to simply explode from sheer boredom. They were only halfway through their meal, but she felt like she'd been sitting at the table for at least six hours.

As Scott twirled some pasta onto his fork and stuffed it into his face, she took another quick peek at Hal's table. He'd finished his dinner at least ten minutes ago but still sat at his table with a book in his hand.

Lust cut through the boredom like a beam of sunlight. How tempting was it to snap a picture of Hal right now? Not to share on that Hot Dudes Reading social media site, but just for her. Something to look at when she was feeling lonely or… horny.

She tamped back her giggles. Would masturbating over a picture of Hal reading give her the title of "Most Pathetic Woman" in the world, or "Most Horniest"? She honestly wasn't sure.

"Savina?"

She dragged her attention back to her date. "Sorry, what was that?"

"I asked how you're enjoying your pasta?" Scott said.

"It's delicious, thanks."

It was delicious, and she for sure would return to this restaurant. Not with Scott, she already knew that she'd never go out with him again after tonight, but maybe she'd do what Hal did and take herself out for dinner. She always felt awkward eating alone, but if she had a book... Hal looked cool eating dinner alone. She could, too, right?

"So, how are the pigs?" Scott asked.

"I'm sorry?"

"The pigs. You raise pigs, right?" he said.

"No. I raise chickens and sell their eggs," she said.

"Right, sorry." Scott smiled apologetically, but his face changed when their server Tabitha stopped at their table. The woman's icy demeanor hadn't thawed one bit. If anything, she seemed even more rage-filled with every visit to their table.

"How is everything?" Tabitha asked.

"Delicious," Savina said brightly. "Thank you."

Tabitha stared at her, and Savina's smile faltered under the pure hatred in her gaze.

"Oh good, I'm so glad," Tabitha said. The venom in her voice made Savina sure Tabitha would be shanking her at some point during the meal.

Tabitha turned to Scott. "And you, sir? How is your meal?"

"It came out a bit cold," Scott said.

"I'll be sure to mention that to the chef," Tabitha said.

"Oh, I'm pretty sure it's an issue of a slow server," Scott said.

Savina stared at him in shock as he pointed to his glass of beer and rudely said, "I'll take another beer."

Okay, forget banging Scott tonight. She'd never let some guy who treated servers this poorly see her lady bits. Fuck that dude.

Tabitha snatched up his half-empty beer. "Of course, sir. Right away, sir."

"Oh, and, Tabitha?" Scott said as she started to walk away. "Maybe try to pour it in a way that I'm not basically paying for foam."

"Scott," Savina said, "don't be a dick."

Before he could reply, Tabitha whirled around to face him, her hand clenched around his drink. "You know what? Maybe we should just get rid of this beer and start fresh."

"Probably for the best," Scott said snottily.

Savina's eyes widened when Tabitha said, "You're just so happy to throw away the best fucking beer of your life and take a new one home, aren't you, Scott?"

"The new beer doesn't nag me all fucking day, Tabitha."

"Maybe if you picked up your fucking socks every once in a while, the old beer wouldn't have to nag you, Scott."

"Maybe if the old beer didn't expect me to say 'how high', the minute she told me to 'jump', I wouldn't be looking for a new beer."

"You asshole!" Tabitha shouted before pouring the half-empty mug of beer directly onto Scott's lap.

Scott jumped to his feet and wiped his hand across his crotch. "Are you fucking kidding me, Tabitha? These are brand new khakis. They cost me fifty bucks!"

"Oh, so suddenly you can spend fifty bucks on pants to look good for your little whore, but I can't hit Sephora's midnight madness sale?"

"That makeup is stupidly expensive!" Scott shouted as

the hum of noise in the restaurant died out, and every single person in the room stared at their table.

"It makes me look pretty!" Tabitha yelled.

"You don't need that stupid make-up shit to be pretty," Scott snapped. "You're fucking gorgeous without it, Tabitha!"

"You think I'm gorgeous?" Tabitha asked.

"Of course I do," Scott said. "You're a fucking knock-out, babe."

"Oh, babe," Tabitha said as she dropped the empty beer glass on the floor. "I miss you so much, babe."

"I miss you too, babe," Scott said. "I wanna come back home."

"I want you to come back home, too," Tabitha said.

Savina's mouth dropped open when Scott yanked Tabitha into his arms, and they kissed passionately.

"Oh God," Savina said when Scott and Tabitha, their tongues slathering across each other's faces and their hands groping and gripping the other's ass, nearly fell onto the table. Savina pushed her chair back when Scott swept their plates and cutlery onto the floor with a loud crash, sending pasta slithering across the floor, before boosting Tabitha onto the table. He dropped onto her, and Tabitha wrapped her legs around his waist as their kissing and moaning grew louder.

A hard hand gripped Savina's arm and pulled her to her feet. She stared at Hal, who said, "Time to go, Savina."

He took her hand, and she grabbed her purse as he linked their fingers together and pushed past the patrons who were starting to gather around the table to watch what, from the sounds of Tabitha and Scott's moans, was about to be a live sex show.

Hal led her out the front door and across the parking lot to her truck.

"You okay?" Hal asked when they stopped next to the driver's door.

Savina burst into laughter. She laughed until her stomach hurt and tears formed in her eyes. Hal leaned against the truck, his arms folded across his chest as he patiently waited for her to finish. Somehow, that only made her laugh harder until finally, her hand on her aching stomach and gasping for breath, she managed to quell the giggles.

"Holy shit, that just happened, right?" she asked.

"Yep," Hal said. "I've had some bad dates, but I've never had a date stick their tongue down our server's throat before."

She laughed, rubbing her aching stomach. "I think they were married or at the very least living together at some point, and I was Scott's revenge date."

"Too bad he couldn't resist Tabitha and how she threw his beer in his face," Hal said.

"His crotch," Savina said with another giggle. "She poured it on his crotch."

Hal laughed, and she couldn't help the tingle that went straight to her pussy. How long had it been since she'd heard Hal laugh? Too long.

"I can't believe I was going to sleep with him," she said. The thought brought on another spat of giggles, and when it ended, she leaned against the truck next to Hal and rubbed at her stomach.

A scowl embedded itself on his face, and she said, "What?"

"Are you drunk?"

"Not yet," she said. "Scott started making out with Tabitha before I could order more wine."

His scowl deepened. "You have to stop going out with strange guys and getting drunk, Savina."

She smiled at him, but all the humour had left her body. "Luckily, I'm an adult who doesn't have to follow your rules."

"Savina –"

She'd planned on apologizing for kissing him at work, but now, she just wanted to go home. She'd send him a card or something. "Good night, Hal."

Without looking at him, she climbed into her truck and shut the door. She turned it on, staring resolutely out the windshield until Hal walked away. She slumped in the seat, rubbing at her forehead. She hated conflict to begin with, but fighting with Hal made her want to barf.

She checked her phone, replying to a message from Harper about what time she should be at Warren's on Saturday, before tossing her phone back into her purse. She drove toward the parking lot exit, slowing to a stop when she saw Hal standing in front of his car with the hood up.

He was bent over the engine, and she stared at his ass for a good thirty seconds before admonishing herself and lowering the window. "Do you know what's wrong with it?"

Hal straightened and slammed the hood shut. "The starter, I think. I'll get Wade to tow it to a garage tomorrow."

"I'll give you a ride home," she said.

"I'll call Warren," he said.

"He's busy finishing up packing. He's moving tomorrow."

"Shit, I forgot," he said. "I'll call Solomon."

She rolled her eyes. "It'll take him twenty minutes to get here from the ranch. I can have you home in ten."

He hesitated for a second longer before nodding. "Okay. Thank you, I appreciate it."

CHAPTER 8

Hal studied his apartment building as Savina parked her truck on the street in front of it. Although it wasn't late, the street was quiet and dark. His neighbourhood wasn't known for loud parties or late-night revelers. Most of his neighbours were like him – people in their late forties or early fifties who kept to themselves.

When he'd first moved here, a couple of years after Mary's death, it had been perfect for him. He was still grieving and didn't want to be friendly with the neighbours. What he wanted was to curl up inside his grief and never leave. He would have, too, if it hadn't been for Alan and Solomon. He owed a lot to his best friends, and he had repaid their kindness with petty jealousy and anger. Thank fucking Christ, he'd internalized it all. Neither of them ever knew how he'd really felt watching them live their lives with Savina and Heather while he grieved for his dead wife.

Yeah, internalizing your feelings has done wonders for you. Asshole.

He ignored his inner voice as Savina shut off her truck. The engine ticked in the quiet, and he unbuckled his seat belt. "Thank you for the ride home."

"You're welcome." Savina stared out the windshield, her hands clasped loosely around the steering wheel.

Hal hesitated. No doubt what he was about to say would lead to another fight, but he had to say it. Savina was putting herself in danger, and it ate him alive with worry.

He sucked in a fortifying breath. "We need to talk, Savina."

Her hands tightened around the steering wheel. "I know. I'm sorry for what I said and did at the clinic. It was beyond inappropriate, and I should have apologized before now."

She looked at him, her cheeks a soft pink and regret shining out from her eyes. "Did I jeopardize your job?"

He stared blankly at her, and she said, "I am happy to speak with Nathan about what he saw. I'm more than willing to tell him it was all my fault and that you shouldn't be punished for –"

"Savina, stop," Hal said. "That isn't what I wanted to talk to you about."

She stared at him in surprise. "It isn't?"

"No. I want to talk about you going on dates and getting drunk."

Irritation flicked across her face. "It isn't any of your business, Hal."

"I know," he said. "This isn't me trying to tell you what to do."

"It sure sounds like it is," she said.

"It's coming from a place of worry," he said. "We're

friends, and I'm worried something bad will happen to you."

"Friends? We haven't been friends for a long time," Savina said. "Unless your idea of friendship is refusing to spend time with me."

That stung like hell, but he didn't try to defend himself or argue. "I'm still worried about you. Getting drunk on dates with men you don't know is dangerous."

"You know why I'm doing it," she said.

"That doesn't make it a good idea."

"I don't care that you're judging me, you know." Her pretty eyes flashed with anger, and her defiant look made him want to kiss her.

"I'm not judging you," he said. "I'm sorry that I'm coming across as judgmental. But I won't apologize for asking you not to get drunk to sleep with someone."

"Yeah, well, it's the only way it's going to happen, so while I appreciate your concern, I'm willing to take the risk."

"You don't have to have sex right now, Savina," Hal said. "You could wait until you don't have to be drunk."

She snorted angry laughter. "I'm so sorry I don't want to live the life of a nun so that you can stop worrying about me. It's my life, and I'll live it the way I want."

"Maybe it's worth exploring with a therapist why you can't even kiss a guy unless you're drunk," Hal said.

"That's not true," Savina said. "I kissed you, and I was stone cold sober that day. You're a great kisser, by the way."

His groin tightened, and he took another deep breath. "Savina, I -"

"Why did you kiss me?" she asked abruptly.

"I think that's obvious," he said.

"Is it? Because I, for one, am confused as fuck," Savina said. "You stopped being my friend because you knew I had a crush on you, but last Saturday, you kissed me and threatened to fuck me right there at the vet clinic. Which, incidentally, was one of the hottest moments of my life."

"I didn't stop being your friend because you had a crush on me. Until Saturday, I had no idea you were attracted to me," he said.

She stared at him before slumping against the seat and rubbing her temples. "Shit. I thought... wait, so that means you're not my friend because of something else. What did I do to make you abandon our friendship, Hal? Whatever it was, it was shitty of you not to explain and give me a chance to apologize."

"It had nothing to do with you," he said. "You didn't do anything."

She stared at him. "Then tell me what it is."

"It doesn't matter," he said.

"Bullshit it doesn't matter. We used to be friends. You were my best friend, Hal. And then you just... stopped. Like I didn't matter to you, like I *never* mattered to you. I thought you were upset by my attraction, thought that the idea of me wanting you made you angry or made you think I was a bad person for betraying Alan. I thought -"

"It was me! Okay? It was all me." His voice was too loud, but Savina didn't flinch.

"What do you mean?"

"I'm attracted to you. I want to fu -I can't be around you anymore because I want to sleep with you and what kind of asshole does that make me?" He banged his fist against his thigh. "It hurt like hell to walk away, and I'm sorry I hurt you, but I didn't know what else to do. That fucking day with that fucking Ikea dresser. If I could go back in time, I -"

"Wait, what did you just say about the Ikea dresser?" Savina asked.

He sighed, forcing his hands to unclench. "That day we built the Ikea dresser for the spare bedroom. That's the day I finally admitted to myself that I wanted to sleep with you."

Savina started to laugh. He watched in silent confusion as she gripped the steering wheel and laughed until tears slid down her cheeks and she wheezed for breath.

"What's so funny?" he asked when she finally got control of herself.

"That was the day I realized I wanted to fuck you," she said and then wheezed out more laughter.

He stared at her. "Are you fucking with me right now?"

She laughed and shook her head. "I'm not, I swear."

"Christ," he said and then banged the back of his head against the headrest several times. "Fucking hell."

"So, now what?" Savina said.

"What do you mean?"

"Well, I'd like to say that we can go back to being friends, but we've tongue licked."

He laughed despite himself. "Tongue licked?"

"I saw it on some tween tv show. Apparently, the term French kissed is only for old people."

"Right," he said.

"Anyway, there's this sexual tension between us, and

unless we do something about it, I'm not sure we can be friends again. At least, not how we used to be."

"And by doing something about it, you mean fucking," Hal said.

She grinned at him, that teasing Savina grin that made him hard as a rock. "I do."

Every part of him wanted to say yes, but he couldn't date Savina. Not when his guilt over Alan's death ate up so much of him. It wasn't fair to saddle her with the shell of the person he used to be.

"I don't want to date you," he said and then muttered a curse. "Shit, that didn't come out the right way. It's just, I'm not -"

"It's fine," she said. "I think we're better off as friends too. But a night of sex could help eliminate the tension between us, right?"

He swallowed hard, hoping his disappointment and hurt weren't a red beacon on his face. Savina was saying what he wanted to hear, but it hurt so goddamn bad to hear her say it.

"It's not a good idea," he said.

She sighed and turned the key in the ignition, her truck starting with a low rumble. "Okay. Good night, Hal."

"Are you going to keep, uh, dating random guys?" he asked.

"If by dating, you mean getting drunk and having sex with a guy for the first time since Alan died, yes," she said.

"Savina -"

"You can't change my mind, Hal. Maybe I'm not ready for a relationship, but I am ready to have sex again."

"If you were, you wouldn't need to be drunk," he said.

"Let's agree to disagree," she said.

Solomon's advice rolling around in his head, he said, "I'll do it."

"Do what?" she asked.

"I'll be the guy you sleep with."

She stared silently at him, and he said, "You just said that if we have sex, it'll end the tension between us. I want to be friends again, Savina. I miss our friendship, and I miss you. If we sleep together, it's a win-win for us. You'll be safe, and I'll get my friend back."

"Okay," she said.

"I know it sounds like I'm just trying to get laid, but I think - wait, what?" Hal stared at Savina.

She smiled at him. "Okay."

He sat back in his seat. "You should take some time and think about it."

"I don't need more time," she said. "I've been attracted to you since last year's great Ikea Desk Incident, remember?"

He smiled a little even though his stomach was swirling with nerves and something else. "I remember."

"Great." She shut off the truck again. "Let's go up to your apartment."

"Savina..."

She stopped with her hand on the door handle, studying the trepidation he knew was evident on his face.

"If you're uncomfortable with me being in your bedroom, I can get us a hotel room," she said quietly.

"What? No, Christ, that isn't a problem for me," he said. "I just... I want you to be absolutely sure this is what you want and clear that this is a one-time thing."

He sounded like an asshole, but it would do no good for either of them to misunderstand what this was.

You really think you can sleep with her once and never again?

He ignored his inner voice with grim determination.

"It is, and I know it's just for tonight," Savina said. "I won't get weird afterward if you don't."

"I won't get weird," he said.

You sure?

"Then we're good to go," she said. "Let's go inside, Hal."

CHAPTER 9

Savina wasn't as nervous as she thought she would be. But she *was* more anxious than she was letting on. She clamped her mouth shut against the barrage of words that wanted to spill from her mouth. Talking too much was a clear indicator of her anxiety, and Hal was well aware of that.

She smiled at him as he hung her jacket in the closet. "Your place looks the same."

She hadn't stepped foot in his apartment for nearly a year.

"Not a lot you can change when you rent," he said. "Come into the kitchen."

She frowned but followed him down the narrow hallway past the half bath to the small kitchen. Hal produced a bottle of whiskey and two glasses, pouring the amber liquid into both before capping the bottle.

She accepted the glass with a nod of thanks. She didn't want a drink. She wanted to be in the bedroom undressing Hal and finally getting a look at that dick she'd fantasized about for the last year, but she sipped politely at it as he drank half of his in a large swallow. Who was she to judge if Hal needed to be drunk to do this?

Still, it sent tendrils of unease skittering through her veins that he needed to drink. She might have needed alcohol to sleep with a stranger, but this was Hal. He knew her better than anyone, and she wasn't lying about him being her best friend.

Her stomach churning, she said, "I know this makes me a hypocrite, but I don't want to do this if you need to be drunk."

Surprise made his eyes widen. "I don't need to be drunk. *You* need to be drunk. Don't you?"

She set the glass on the counter. "Not with you."

A look flickered across his face. One she couldn't decipher despite how well she knew him.

"You okay?" she asked.

"Yes." He set his glass next to hers and hesitated before stepping close and sliding his arm around her waist. He studied her in the bright light of the kitchen, then brushed his mouth against hers.

His gentleness made her pelvis ache pleasantly. She returned his kiss, parting her lips encouragingly. He pulled back instead of deepening the kiss. "We can sit on the couch for a while. We don't have to go directly to the bedroom."

"I'm good with the bedroom," she said. "Unless you have a sex on the couch fantasy you're trying to make happen."

He laughed, and she had to blink back the sudden tears. God, she'd missed him so much the last year.

He took her hand, and she followed him to his

bedroom. He turned on the bedside lamp and studied her in the dim circle of light. "You're sure, Savina?"

"Yes," she said without a moment of hesitation. "I want this, Hal. I want *you*."

"I want you too." His voice was warm like melting honey, and she reached for his shirt, tugging it over his head when he raised his arms.

He had a good body, an amazing body, in fact, and desire descended in a heavy wave that made her feel a little lightheaded. She traced her fingers through his salt and pepper chest hair, listening to his sharp inhale of breath when she moved further down to his flat stomach.

His hands gripped her hips and pulled her against him. She rubbed against his erection, and he groaned, the sound sending goosebumps popping up against her skin.

She kissed him, draping her arms over his shoulders as they leisurely explored each other's mouths. The ache grew in her belly, and she was drowning in a deep, heady desire she hadn't felt in too long.

Hal's hands moved to her ass and squeezed, pulling her up even more firmly against his erection. She ground against it as they broke apart, sucked in oxygen, and dove back into the kiss.

Hal swept his tongue across hers, and when she slid her tongue into his mouth, he sucked hard on it. She clutched at his shoulders, moaning her disappointment when he broke the kiss and rested his forehead against hers. They both breathed like they'd just scaled a mountain and her heartbeat thundered in her ears.

"You're amazing at kissing," she said.

"You too," he said, but his voice was distracted, and his gaze was trained on her breasts.

She smiled and leaned back enough to pull her t-shirt over her head and drop it on the floor. Hal sucked in a harsh breath and immediately cupped her right breast through her bra, running his thumb over her nipple until it hardened.

She reached behind her and unclasped her bra. Hal slid the straps down over her arms, and she let the bra drop to the floor with her shirt. Her breasts were her best feature, but they weren't nearly as perky as they were in her youth, and she had a moment of self-doubt. It quickly disappeared at the look of awe that crossed Hal's face.

"So fucking beautiful," he murmured before cupping her breast in his big, rough hand.

She moaned, her back arching a little when he teased her aching nipple before plucking at it with his finger and thumb. "Hal!"

His cocky grin only made her want him more. She reached for his belt, unbuckling it before popping open the button on his jeans and yanking down the zipper. She slipped her hand beneath his briefs, a smug smile crossing her face when she wrapped her fingers around his thick-ness, and he groaned loudly.

She stroked him firmly, swiping her thumb through the moisture at his tip before bringing her hand to her mouth and sucking it clean.

"Fucking hell, Savina," Hal growled and reached for her pants. He unbuttoned them and shoved them down to mid-thigh. They dragged her panties with them, and she reached for her underwear, her cheeks flaming bright red.

"No," Hal said, taking both her wrists and pinning them behind her back with one hard hand. "I want to see your gorgeous pussy."

Her cheeks went even hotter, and she tugged experimentally at Hal's hold. Her pussy grew shamefully wetter when he tightened his grip and shook his head again. "Stay still."

She closed her eyes, her body trembling against Hal as he smoothed his hand over the curve of her belly before stroking the front of her thighs. "Spread your legs for me."

She did what he demanded, parting them as much as her jeans would allow. A breathless moan escaped her lips when he toyed with her pubic hair and then skimmed his fingers over her wet pussy lips.

The pad of his finger slipped between her lips and circled her clit. She cried out, arching against Hal and yanking at his grip. "Hal, please!"

He let her go, and she grabbed his shoulders, squeezing tight as she stared into his gaze. A second finger joined the first, and she pumped her hips against his touch as he stroked and caressed her swollen clit.

Shamefully, she was already close, and she made a low moan of need, her fingers digging into his bare flesh. "Oh God, Hal. I'm... I'm going to come."

He smiled, and his arm anchored around her waist, pulling her tight against him as he rubbed her clit firmly. "Show me."

"Fuck," she moaned. Her legs trembled, and she leaned into Hal, trusting him to hold her weight as she chased her climax. His fingers were firm against her clit, rubbing in relentless circles that brought waves of delicious pleasure.

The pleasure coiled deep in her pelvis, her nipples tightened, and she buried her face in Hal's neck as her orgasm washed over her. She barely heard Hal's soft sound of approval over her loud cries of ecstasy. She shook in

Hal's grip, drowning in the pleasure of her orgasm as he stopped rubbing her oversensitive clit and palmed her pussy. Her pulse thudding and body still shaking, she allowed Hal to help her onto the bed, collapsing on her back and numbly watching as he pulled off her pants, underwear, and socks before removing the rest of his clothes.

His cock stood straight up, the head a dark red and covered in precum as it brushed against his flat abdomen.

"Pretty," she breathed out.

Hal smiled, stroking her thigh with one warm hand as he opened the nightstand drawer with the other. He grabbed a box of condoms and hesitated before flipping it over to study the bottom. "Shit."

"What?" she asked.

"They're expired."

She grinned. "How long since you've had sex, Hal?"

"Over a year," he said.

She studied him for a few seconds before saying, "You know I haven't had sex with anyone in three years, and I know you've had a vasectomy, so..."

"My last STI test was negative," he said, "but we don't have to have sex tonight if -"

"Yes, we do," she said. "I'm fine not using a condom."

The relief on his face made her giggle, which she supposed wasn't very sexy, but she couldn't help it. "Get in the bed, handsome."

He tugged lightly on her thigh. "Open for me."

A fresh wave of need washed over her at his tone - she liked bossy Hal a great deal - and let her legs fall open as Hal knelt between them. He rubbed her inner thighs, studying her pussy intently until she squirmed self-consciously and started to close her thighs. "Hal, I -"

He pushed her thighs apart again with those hard hands of his, holding her open wide for his perusal. "Shh. Let me look at your pretty pussy."

She swallowed hard, her hands digging into the sheets as Hal stroked his dick with one hand while he traced her pussy with his other hand. "Fuck, this pussy is so gorgeous."

She yelped in surprise when he hooked his arms around her thighs and yanked her closer until her ass was nearly sitting on his thighs, and she was flat on her back. He smiled at her as he guided his cock to her opening and pressed the head against her. "Ready for me?"

"Yes," she breathed.

He pressed forward, holding her legs firmly, and his gaze trained on her pussy as he fed his cock into her inch by inch. She squirmed, her pussy protesting at the foreign invasion, and Hal made a soothing sound but didn't stop pressing forward.

"Hal," she moaned. "I need a minute."

He stopped immediately, rubbing her thighs as he studied his cock, only half-buried in her pussy. "Breathe, Savina."

"I am," she said grumpily, making Hal laugh. She sucked in a deep breath. "Christ, I should have been using a dildo the last few years."

He rubbed her thighs and pushed forward another inch, his dick relentless in its quest to be buried in her. "You don't use toys?"

"I have a mini-vibe I use for my clit sometimes," she panted, groaning when Hal gave her another inch of dick.

He made his own groan. "Fuck, you're so wet and tight. Relax for me."

"I am relaxed," she said.

He rubbed her clit with his thumb, and she gasped at the unexpected pleasure, her hips bucking forward to meet his touch. Her pussy took the last of his dick, and they both moaned.

Hal rubbed her thighs roughly, staring at her pussy as he made a few slow thrusts. "Christ, you feel so good."

He pushed her legs up, pressing his hands against her thighs. "Put your hands behind your knees, Savina."

She did what he asked, her face flushing when he pushed her legs apart until she felt the strain in her thigh muscles. "Good, keep your legs spread wide for me."

He moved in and out of her, long, hard thrusts of his dick that made her toes curl and her pelvis ache. He kept his gaze trained on her pussy, one hard hand flat against her belly to hold her in place as he fucked her.

Her legs were starting to ache, and her arms shook from exertion, but when she tried to lower her legs, Hal shook his head and gave her a stern look that made her squirm with unexpected pleasure. "No, keep them up and open for me."

His voice was hard and demanding, nothing like his usual easygoing nature, and hot desire took her breath away. She liked this version of Hal, liked it very much, and so did her pussy, apparently.

Hal grinned in satisfaction, no doubt he could feel the hot rush of liquid that had flooded her pussy, and pumped harder in and out of her. "You feel so fucking good, Savina. Your pussy is hot and tight and perfect."

He rubbed the back of her thigh with one hand and her

clit with the other. "A pussy this tight should be fucked every day. I want to fuck it every day, want to have you underneath me, want to watch your pussy take my dick over and over while you beg me to come."

"Oh my God," she moaned, her hips moving like a piston to keep up with Hal's suddenly hard, rough thrusts.

She'd never once imagined Hal to be a dirty talker in bed, never once thought he would be an alpha or dom or whatever the fuck the younger generation called it. Now that she knew and was being fucked by this unexpected version of Hal, she'd never be able to look at him the same way again. Not when what he was saying, what he was *doing*, was making her hotter than fire.

His face a mask of dark need, Hal fucked her harder, driving into her over and over until the bed squeaked and the headboard banged against the wall.

His neighbours will complain, she thought hazily before Hal's thumb rubbed against her clit, and she ceased to think rationally. There was only the feel of Hal's hardness in her softness, his thumb stroking her aching clit, the sound of his harsh pants and low groans as she took everything he gave her.

She cried his name when her second orgasm burst through her in a flash of heat and bright light. He groaned as her pussy tightened around him, and he thrust into her one last time, his entire body shuddering as he emptied himself into her.

She twitched in surprise, the last of her climax still making her shake with pleasure when he pulled out of her and rubbed his dick roughly. A final few ropes of white cum splattered against her lower belly, and she stared into Hal's hot gaze as he smeared his seed into her skin.

Hal collapsed on his side beside her, breathing hard. She touched her sticky skin, but when she reached for the sheet to wipe her stomach, he pushed her hand away and pulled the sheet and quilt up over their bodies. "Leave it."

"You came on me," she said.

He nodded. "I did."

"Is that, like, a kink for you?"

He just shrugged, and she turned to face him, tucking one hand under the pillow. "Are you that guy?"

"That guy?" He arched an eyebrow at her.

"You know, a guy who wants to come all over my face as some kind of power trip."

He shook his head. "No, if my dick is that close to your face, I expect you to swallow my cum like a good girl."

Her mouth dropped open. "Holy fuck, you're a kinky son of a bitch."

He laughed so hard that the bed frame rattled against the wall.

She grinned happily at him, and he cupped her hip, sliding closer until their bodies touched. "I'll only come on your face if you ask me nicely."

She rolled her eyes, and he reached around to give her ass an affectionate squeeze. "In all seriousness, I would never come on a woman's face without asking permission first. And if you dislike what I just did, I won't do it again."

"I didn't dislike it," she said. "It was just... unexpected."

He rubbed her hip without saying anything. He had an adorably sleepy look on his face, and when he yawned, she couldn't help but yawn too. She hadn't slept well the last few nights, and the temptation to snuggle up against Hal and spend the night was hard to resist.

She made a motion to sit up, and Hal's arm tightened around her waist. "Where are you going?"

"I wasn't sure if I should leave or -"

"Stay the night," he said. "It's cold and too late for you to drive home."

She checked the alarm clock on the nightstand. It was only a little after ten, but she didn't argue. Instead, she gave in to what she wanted and snuggled in close. Hal reached over her to shut off the light, and then they moved and shifted, situating legs and arms until they were both comfortable with their legs entwined and their breaths mingling.

It was nice to be in a man's arms again, under a warm quilt in a comfortable bed, listening to the wind rattling outside.

"Hal?"

"Hmm?" He was half asleep.

"Thank you."

A small smile crossed his face, and he pressed a gentle kiss against her mouth. "Go to sleep, Savina."

CHAPTER 10

Hal parked his bike next to Harper's piece of shit car and killed the engine. He got off the bike and set his helmet on the seat before glancing at the sky. It was a beautiful October day, and the decision to take his bike to Warren's was easy. He wouldn't have much longer to ride the bike before the snow fell, and he'd take advantage of every opportunity he could.

He studied the extra helmet strapped to the back seat. He hadn't put the helmet on there this morning for any particular reason. It certainly wasn't because he wanted to be prepared if Savina wanted to ride. He wasn't stupid. He'd seen the disappointment on her face when he didn't take her home on the bike the night of her disastrous date at the Beaver.

About six months after Alan died, she'd been having a terrible day and desperate to help her manage her grief, Hal had suggested a bike ride. Savina had never been on a motorcycle before, but she'd been instantly hooked after just one ride.

He pulled off his gloves and set them next to his helmet. He'd taken her on plenty of rides over the following two years, just as delighted as Savina was at how much she'd loved it. Mary had tolerated the bike riding, but it had never been her thing, and he could count on one hand the number of times he'd gotten her on the back of his bike.

The bike rides with Savina had been just one of many things he'd missed the last year. He rubbed the back of his neck and made his way past the multiple vehicles parked in the driveway of Warren's house. He didn't see Savina's truck and worry rocketed through him. She was supposed to be here. Had something happened to her?

The front door opened, and Savina appeared carrying a large cardboard box. She wore her usual t-shirt and jeans, with her hair in a high ponytail. As she carefully walked up the ramp into the U-Haul parked near the front door, Hal leaned against Warren's SUV. The rapid beating of his heart could only partially be blamed on his relief that she was okay.

Shit, this was gonna be harder than he thought.

Just don't make it weird.

He grimaced. Savina had already made it weird by sneaking out of his apartment sometime between when they'd fallen asleep and when Hal woke at his usual six thirty. He grimaced and scrubbed his hand over his face, ignoring his instinct to duck behind the SUV when Savina came out of the U-Haul.

To his relief, she didn't look his way, just continued into the house. He studied her perfect ass, hating that it made him half-hard even though he knew he'd never be with her again.

He wouldn't say that last night had been a mistake, being with Savina had been everything he'd ever dreamed it could be, but the guilt he felt was a heavy weight that felt impossible to carry.

Did Savina carry that same guilt? Was that why she'd left without waking him?

He was pretty sure the answer was yes, and that fucking gutted him. Savina shouldn't and didn't deserve to have any guilt.

He hurried forward when Harper and the owner of Red Door Tattoo shop walked out of the door, balancing an empty bookshelf between them.

"Harper, let me help with that." Hal slid his hands around the bookshelf, taking its weight as Harper stepped back.

"Thank you, Hal."

Moving carefully, they loaded the bookshelf into the U-Haul, sliding it in next to a second bookshelf and a stack of boxes.

Harper had followed them into the U-Haul, and she shifted one of the boxes into a more secure spot before smiling at him. "Hal, have you met Addie's boyfriend, Preacher? He owns the tattoo shop on Main Street. "

Addie was Addison Moore, a schoolteacher and Harper's best friend since they were kids.

Hal shook Preacher's hand. The big man had a firm grip and a 'don't fuck with me' vibe that was a direct contrast to Addie's sweet and gentle nature. Still, there must have been a strong connection between them. Addison's name was tattooed on Preacher's forearm in a large, thick font.

"Nice to meet you," Hal said.

"You too," Preacher said.

"Hal is a vet tech at the clinic," Harper said to Preacher. "The best vet tech at the clinic, which makes it a bit of a miracle that Nathan gave him the Saturday off to help Dad move."

"Jade and Allie are just as good as me," Hal said.

"So not true." Harper slid her arm around his waist and squeezed affectionately as Preacher walked down the ramp of the U-haul and headed into the house. "Thank you for helping today."

"Sorry I'm late," he said. "The starter went on my car last night, and I had to deal with getting it towed this morning."

"Shit, that sucks. But you're not even late." Harper followed him down the ramp and toward the house. "Kira and Conner were here early, so we started early. Addie and Preacher and Aunt Savina just got here five minutes ago."

He tried not to stiffen at Savina's name but must have done a piss poor job of it because Harper said, "What's wrong?"

"Nothing." He opened the screen door, stopping so quickly when he saw Savina right there with another box that Harper bumped into the back of him.

"Oof," Harper said. "What's happening up there?" She peered around him. "Hey, Savina."

"Hi, sweetie." Savina glanced at him quickly before looking away. "Hello, Hal."

"Hi, Savina."

After an awkward silence, Savina said, "Excuse me," and squeezed past him and out the door.

Hal ignored his urge to readjust his dick which hadn't

failed to notice the brief brush of Savina's ass against it as she moved past him.

Harper popped up in front of him with suspicion written all over her face. "Did you and Savina fight?"

"Of course not," he said.

"You act like you're fighting," Harper said.

"Who's fighting?" Warren ducked his head into the hallway from the living room. "Hal! Thanks again for helping today."

"No problem." Hal moved past Harper and clapped Warren on the shoulder. "Where should I start?"

SAVINA LEANED AGAINST THE WALL BEFORE SLIDING DOWN it and plopping on her butt next to a sweaty and red-faced Harper. "How are you doing, sweetie?"

"I'm hot, I can't stop sweating, and," Harper sniffed her armpits, "I freaking smell. Thank God Nathan is working at the clinic. We haven't been dating long enough for him to see me like this."

Savina laughed. "Nathan is adorably in love with you. I doubt a little sweat and stink is gonna scare him off."

Harper grinned. "I mean, I am pretty great, right?"

Savina slung her arm around Harper's narrow shoulders and kissed the top of her head. "You are. And I'm only partially saying that because you're related to me."

Harper laughed, and Savina tugged on one short pink-coloured lock of Harper's hair. "But seriously, are you okay? I know it has to be hard seeing your childhood home packed up like this."

There was a soft woof and Harper's dog, an old shepherd cross named Winston, limped into the living room. He laid down beside Harper and rested his head in her lap. She stroked his head, smiling at the way his tail wagged.

"It's a little difficult, but the fact that I'll still be living here with Nathan makes it much easier to accept." Harper stared around the empty room. "Before I got together with Nathan, and even for a bit afterward, I was upset that Dad had sold the house to Nathan as part of the clinic purchase. I mean, it made sense since it's right next door to the vet clinic, but still… it was hard to fathom Dad not being here, you know?"

"I do," Savina said.

"But I think Dad will be much happier living in town in the condo. He's as excited as a little kid about his new place," Harper said.

"I think so, too," Savina said.

They sat silently for a minute or so before Harper said, "Are you and Hal fighting?"

"No," Savina said. "Hey, how is the new vet Nathan hired working out?"

"Dr. Yale is doing well. She's only been at the clinic for a week, but Nathan says she's smart, confident, and great with the clients - both human and animal ones."

"Your dad said she's fairly new, just graduated last year?" Savina said.

"I think so." Harper poked her in the arm. "Stop changing the subject. What's going on with you and Hal?"

"Nothing," Savina said.

"Horseshit," Harper said, sounding so much like Warren that Savina couldn't help but laugh. "What did you fight about?"

"We didn't fight, we -" She cut herself off abruptly.

She couldn't tell Harper she slept with Hal. She was close with her niece but not 'share details of her intimate life' close.

"Oh my God," Harper squinted at her and lowered her voice. "You slept with him."

Savina's mouth dropped open, and she didn't have a chance in hell of denying it. Still, she gave it the old college try. "I... no, we didn't."

Harper rolled her eyes. "I'm not a little kid, Savina. I recognize an "I fucked a guy, and now I regret it' look when I see one. I saw it on my own face a few times before I met Nathan."

"I don't regret it," Savina said.

Harper studied her and then nodded. "Good. You shouldn't. So, why are things so weird between you now?"

"Because it happened last night, and I sneaked out of his house at four this morning while he was sleeping."

"Yikes," Harper said. "No wonder he's been avoiding you all day."

"He's pissed at me," Savina said with a sigh. Her stomach churned. Upsetting Hal made her feel like a real asshole. Hell, she *was* an asshole. A confused, well-meaning asshole, but still an asshole.

"No, he isn't," Harper said. "I've known Hal since I was a little kid, and he doesn't have his pissed-off look. It's more of a 'kicked puppy' look."

"That makes me feel worse," Savina said.

"Sorry, honey." Now it was Harper's turn to put her arm around Savina. "Why did you leave?"

"It's complicated," Savina glanced at the open door-way, "and this probably isn't the best time to try to explain."

"Fair enough," Harper said. "But I'll tell Dad that I'll drive you home, and we can -"

"Harper?" Addie walked into the living room. She wore sweatpants and a t-shirt, and her auburn hair was pulled into a neat bun on top of her head. She wore no makeup, but her skin was flawless, and she looked like she was breezing in from a day spent at the spa rather than lifting and moving heavy boxes all day.

"Oh my God," Harper said with a good-natured scowl. "Can you please explain to me why we did an equal amount of carrying boxes today, and yet, you look like a freaking sun goddess, and I look like a lumpy, sweaty cobweb monster?"

Addie laughed. "Don't be ridiculous. You look gorgeous."

"I don't smell gorgeous," Harper said.

"That's for sure," Savina said.

"Hey!" Harper said as Addie laughed again.

"Your dad sent me in here to find you. Connor and Preacher have loaded the last of the boxes into the U-Haul. Can you come outside?"

"Help me up," Harper said, holding her hands out. Addie grabbed her hands and hauled her to her feet.

Harper took Savina's hand and helped her up. "C'mon, gorgeous."

The three of them joined the others in the front yard. Warren stood next to the U-Haul, the setting sun sending beams of cold light across the yard.

Hal leaned against the U-Haul beside Warren with his arms folded across his chest. He'd stripped off his hoodie, and Savina studied how his t-shirt pulled across his chest. A memory of that hard chest, of the salt and pepper hair that covered it, wormed its way into her head. She looked away, her cheeks turning hot as her lady bits sat up and demanded another go at Hal's thick cock.

"I can't say thank you enough for all your help today," Warren said. "It's much appreciated, and I'd like to take you to The Pizza Stone for pizza and cold beer."

"Can I sneak in on that?" Nathan had joined them, jogging across the small footbridge that crossed the small creek between the vet clinic and Warren's house. He went to put his arms around Harper, and she pressed a hand against his chest.

"You might not want to get too close until after I shower," she said.

He grinned at her and pulled her into his embrace. "You smell great to me."

"Lies, all lies," she said with a cute grin before patting his butt.

"Yes, you can join us," Warren said. "There will be plenty of food."

"But only because you're helping unload the U-Haul tomorrow. Otherwise, you'd have to just sit there and watch me eat pizza and drink beer," Harper said with a teasing grin.

Warren rolled his eyes before rummaging in his pocket for keys. "Let's head out."

"I need to pass on the invite," Savina said. "I'm pretty tired, and I should get home and check on Izzie and the puppies."

"You sure?" Warren asked.

She nodded. "Yes. I'll see you tomorrow at the condo around nine?"

Warren smiled gratefully at her. "Sounds good. Thank you."

He turned to the others. "I'll drive Savina home and meet you at the restaurant."

"Don't worry about it. I'll get an Uber," Savina said.

"I'll drive her home, Dad," Harper said, "and then come by the restaurant."

"I don't think your car will make it to Savina's and back," Nathan said. "Take my truck."

Savina shook her head. "No, don't worry about it. I'll take an Uber home. It's not that far."

"Don't be silly," Harper said. "You're not paying for an Uber when one of us can drive you home."

"It's not a big deal. I don't -"

"I'll drive Savina home." Hal's low voice made her stomach do crazy flip flops. "I have plans for tonight, so I can't make the restaurant. I'll drop her off at home before I head out."

Savina stared desperately at Harper, who quickly said, "You don't want to be late for your plans. I don't mind driving her home."

"It won't make me late." Hal stared at Savina, his gaze nearly turning her thighs to liquid and making her nipples tighten. "As long as you're good with riding the bike?"

Happiness lit her up like a rocket. "You brought your bike?"

He nodded, and her traitorous mouth said, "Okay, well, sure, if you're sure you don't mind."

"I'm sure," Hal said.

"Okay, then it's settled. Hal, get my baby sister home safe, and I'll see the rest of you at the restaurant," Warren said.

Savina couldn't hide her excitement as she followed Hal to his bike. The others were piling into various vehicles, and she waved to Harper as she and Nathan drove by them. She studied Hal's bike with genuine affection, reaching out to run her hand along the seat as Hal unstrapped the extra helmet.

"She looks good," Savina said.

Hal put on the leather jacket draped across the seat before looking her up and down. His gaze didn't linger on her chest or hips, and she swallowed her disappointment as he turned and rummaged in one of the saddlebags before pulling out a second, worn-looking leather jacket. "You won't be warm enough in just your t-shirt."

She took the jacket with a nod of thanks, shrugging into it and zipping it up as Hal put on his helmet and then handed her the second one. It wasn't the one he'd bought for her. That one was at home, safely tucked away in her closet in a box where she didn't have to look at it every day and feel that ache of loss.

She slipped the helmet on and buckled it before turning on the intercom.

"Ready?" Hal had already climbed onto the bike, and she swung her leg over, sitting on the seat behind him. It'd been over a year since she'd been in this exact spot, and it felt a little like coming home. She put her feet on the pegs and slid her arms around Hal's waist, clasping her hands across his flat stomach and sliding close until her knees squeezed his narrow hips, and she was flat against his back.

God, she'd missed this.

The bike started with a smooth rumble, and she excitedly squeezed Hal's waist.

"You okay?" His voice came through the intercom.

"Yes," she said. "I'm good to go."

She could hear the impatience in her voice, and Hal obviously could as well because he made a low chuckle and said, "Hang on tight, sweet Savina."

CHAPTER 11

Savina slid off the back of Hal's bike, pulling off her helmet and setting it on the seat as Hal shut off the bike and removed his helmet.

"Thank you so much," she said. Her cheeks hurt from how wide her smile was. "That was amazing."

He grinned at her. "Glad you enjoyed it."

"I really did."

He glanced at her truck sitting in the driveway. "Are you having vehicle problems?"

"No. Valerie Tapp came by this morning and asked if she could borrow it for the day. She needed to take some furniture to Goodwill, and Victor got their truck in the divorce settlement. I knew I could take an Uber to Warren's, so I said sure."

Hal shook his head, a small smile on his face. "So you spend your own money to help out a neighbour."

She shrugged. "She's struggling right now. Victor was a real douchebag about splitting assets, and he made her buy the house from him to stay in it. I know money is tight for her, and borrowing my truck saves her from hiring someone to haul it away. And it's not like I don't have enough money."

She unzipped Hal's jacket. Selling the eggs from her hens gave her a nice nest egg - pun intended - but it wasn't enough to survive. However, their farm had long since been paid for, and the life insurance cheque she'd received after Alan died was more than enough to give her a comfortable life.

She smiled a little. Alan had been insistent early in their marriage about having life insurance policies for both of them. His practicality was only one of the many things she'd loved about him.

She handed Hal the jacket. "Thank you for the ride home, Hal. I really enjoyed it. I've missed riding you."

Her cheeks went beet red as realization flashed over her. "I mean with you. Riding *with* you."

Hal's grin made her pussy ache with need even as more embarrassment washed over her.

After a beat of silence, he said, "How is Izzie doing?"

"Much better. Still on antibiotics, but I think the UTI is almost cleared up. Do you want to come in and see her and the puppies?"

"Sure," he said.

She hid her surprise. She hadn't expected Hal to say yes, but she was glad he had. It would give her a chance to spend a little more time with him and apologize for sneaking out this morning.

She grabbed the keys from the visor and locked the truck as Hal packed away his extra jacket and strapped down the second helmet before leaving his on the seat. He followed her inside the house, leaving his boots at the door and hanging his jacket on the coat tree.

She flicked on the light in the kitchen as Izzie walked out of the dining room, her tail wagging happily. She sat in front of Savina, and Savina gave her a few soft scratches around her ears. "Hi, Izzie girl. Did you have a good day, sweet mama?"

At the sound of Savina's voice, a chorus of high-pitched whining came from the dining room. Hal grinned as she winced and said, "I love the babies, but my God, they can be so loud."

Hal petted Izzie, squatting down to rub her belly when she rolled over. "Let's go see your babies, Izzie."

Savina led him toward the dining room. Two years ago, she'd turned it into a full-time puppy nursery by removing all the furniture and turning a big chunk of it into a whelping pen with low wooden walls that puppies couldn't climb out of, but a mama could jump in and out to feed her babies. Hal had helped her set it up, and his experience as a vet tech and former dog foster was invaluable.

The babies' yelping and hollering grew louder as they entered the nursery. Savina glanced into the pen and sighed. While Izzie could use the doggie door to do her business, the puppies were contained in their nursery. After being gone all day, the puppy pen was in dire need of cleaning.

She smiled at Hal as he picked up one of the puppies and snuggled it against his chest. "They're getting so big."

"Izzie's done a great job nursing them," Savina said. The puppy licked Hal's face enthusiastically, and she felt a moment of actual envy. She wanted to be licking Hal. Repeatedly.

When Hal set the puppy back in the pen, she grimaced. "Well, you've got puppy poop on you now."

He stared at the poop footprint on his shirt and laughed. "It won't be the first or the last, not in my line of work."

"I really need to clean the pen. While I clean, I let the puppies roam free in the dining room if you want to get in some cuddles," Savina said.

"I'll help you clean the pen," Hal said.

"You don't have to do that," Savina said. "You clean enough kennels at work. You don't need to do it during your free time."

"I don't mind," Hal said. "It'll go faster if I help."

Before she could argue, Hal stepped into the pen and started scooping the puppies up and depositing them on the other side of the pen. She ran to close the door to the dining room as the puppies immediately scattered across the room to chase Izzie and wrestle with each other.

"Hal, are you sure?" Savina said.

"Positive." He grinned at her. "Grab those pee pads, and let's do this."

"THANK YOU FOR YOUR HELP. I REALLY APPRECIATE IT." Savina peeked through the half-open door of the dining room. Izzie was curled up in the freshly cleaned pen, the babies nursing contently against her.

"You're welcome." Hal stood behind her, his warm breath against her neck as he studied the babies. "How much longer will you be fostering them?"

"Not too much longer. They'll be weaned soon, and

Rayna has already lined up some new foster homes for them."

Rayna was Rayna Abrams, a local plumber and the founder of Little Whiskers Rescue.

"What about Izzie?" Hal asked.

"I'll keep fostering her until she's adopted. What time is your thing tonight?" Savina walked toward the kitchen. She needed to put some space between Hal and her before she did something crazy like fuck him right there in the hallway.

Hal followed her and leaned against the counter, staring blankly at her. "My thing?"

"Your plans," she said as she washed her hands with the hand soap next to the sink and dried them.

As Hal washed his hands, she opened the fridge and grabbed water for both of them. "You said you couldn't go to the restaurant because you had plans."

"Right. Uh," faint red coloured his cheeks, "that might not have been entirely true."

She grinned at him. "If Harper finds out you lied about having plans, she'll probably steal your figurine collection and hold them for ransom."

He laughed. "Probably."

She hesitated and then crossed the kitchen to open a far drawer. "Speaking of which."

She handed him the small bison figurine, her stomach weirdly nervous. "I found this a few months ago at a thrift store in Riverton. You probably already have it, but I bought it just in case you didn't."

He took the bison from her, and the look of delight on his face calmed her stomach. Hal had collected the vintage Wade figurines for as long as she'd known him, and his impressive collection was displayed in a glass cabinet in his living room. She didn't remember seeing the bison, but it had been a while since she'd seen his collection.

"I don't have this one. It's from the Animal Series One, and it's the only one I'm missing from that series," he said.

She took a drink of water. "Well, I'm super happy I bought it for you."

He studied her. "I am too. Thank you for thinking of me even when we weren't…."

"Friends anymore?"

"Talking as much," he said.

She picked at the water bottle label as awkward silence made the kitchen air feel thick like molasses. She needed to apologize for last night and could no longer put it off.

"Hal, I'm sorry for leaving without saying goodbye this morning." She risked a glance at him, surprised by the compassion on his face. "It was a shitty thing of me to do."

"I understand." He set the figurine on the counter and took a drink of water.

She frowned. She should have been happy that Hal was so understanding. Instead, she was confused as hell. "Why aren't you angry with me?"

"Because I'm not an asshole," he said.

"What's that supposed to mean?"

He sighed. "I'm not going to be angry because you feel guilty about sleeping with me."

"I don't feel guilty," she said.

Exasperation crossed his face. "Lying about your guilt isn't healthy. You shouldn't -"

"I'm not lying," she said, her cursedly short temper already rising to the surface. She took a deep breath. "Well, mostly. Look, I didn't feel guilty about sleeping with you, at least not in the way you assume. I woke up around three and couldn't get back to sleep, and then my stupid brain started overthinking and I realized my lack of guilt actually made me feel guilty. I laid there in the dark wondering what kind of person I was to be so guilt free about sleeping with you, and then I started worrying that you might feel guilty or regret it. That made me feel awful and confused, and the idea of seeing that regret on your face when you woke up panicked me, so I snuck out of your house like a giant chicken."

She set her water on the counter. "But it was immature and selfish of me to do that to you, and I want to say I'm sorry."

"Apology accepted," Hal said.

Relief washed over her, and she sagged against the counter. "Thank you for being so understanding."

He nodded, and she dragged her nail over a scratch in the countertop. "It was good between us, wasn't it?"

"Yes," he said bluntly. "Really good."

"Yeah." She gathered her courage, reminding herself to keep her damn feelings off her face if his answer destroyed her. "Are you... I mean... do you regret it?"

He stared directly at her before moving so close his chest nearly brushed hers. "I have no regrets about being with you, Savina."

She needed to ask him if he felt guilty, but did she really want to know the answer when he was standing so close to her? When she could lean forward and kiss him if she wanted? When it'd been less than twenty-four hours since she'd been with him, but she already wanted him again with a fierceness that shocked her?

"Hal," she whispered.

He reached out and brushed back a strand of hair that had escaped her ponytail and clung to her cheek. "Savina."

"I know we said only once, but I want you again."

His gaze fell to her mouth. "I want you again too."

"Maybe just once more to help with the tension?" she said.

"Once more would probably be very helpful to ease the tension." He let his mouth hover over hers, those perfect lips tempting her into madness.

"So helpful," she breathed before pressing her mouth against his.

He palmed the back of her skull, pulling her tight against him as they kissed. Kissing Hal was a delicious, addictive drug. He explored her mouth with a slow and tender style that had her clinging to him and making small cries and whimpers for more.

When Hal slipped his hand under her shirt and cupped her breast through her sports bra, she was suddenly too aware of what she'd been doing all day and how much she'd been sweating. Not to mention they'd just finished cleaning a puppy pen.

She pulled back, breaking their kiss.

"What's wrong?" Hal asked, his hand stilling on her breast.

"Nothing. Other than we both spent the day sweating like crazy, and we just finished cleaning up a truly epic amount of puppy poop."

Hal grinned. "You make a good point."

"I can have a quick shower and then make us some sandwiches while you shower," she said.

"Or," Hal squeezed her ass, "we could shower together

and then have a bite to eat after we fuck each other's brains out."

"As long as you promise not to fizzle out halfway through the fucking because of lack of food," she said.

Hal's low chuckle sent a rush of liquid straight to her pussy. "I promise."

CHAPTER 12

She took his hand and led him to the attached bathroom in her bedroom. She flicked on the light, and Hal said, "Holy shit."

"You like?" She grinned at him. "I had it renovated earlier this year."

"It's amazing," he said.

"I've always wanted a walk-in double shower." She opened the shower door and turned on both showerheads, adjusting the temperature before shutting the door. "It seems a little excessive for one person, I guess, but sometimes I turn on both showerheads even when it's just me in there."

He grinned at her as he stripped off his shirt. "Nothing wrong with indulging yourself a little."

"That's what I thought." She pulled off her clothes, surprisingly not feeling even a little self-conscious in the bright light of the bathroom.

She took Hal's hand and led him into the shower when they were both naked. They stood side-by-side under the showerheads, letting the hot water run over them. Hal dipped his head under the spray before smiling at her. "This is incredible."

"Right?" She wet her hair and reached for the shampoo, handing it over to Hal without protest when he tugged it from her hands.

He washed her hair with gentle efficiency. She rinsed her hair clean and then returned the favour, kneading Hal's scalp until he groaned in pleasure. When he'd rinsed the shampoo away, he lathered his hands with soap and pulled her close, running his soapy hands over her shoulders.

"You know, I've been washing myself since I was a little kid," she teased.

His hands slipped to her breasts, turning her nipples into soapy little points as her hips arched and his erection pressed against her stomach.

"It's always nice to have help, don't you think?" Hal kissed her wet neck, nipping at her skin as his hands caressed and cleaned her upper body before he lathered more soap and slipped his hand between her legs. He washed her pussy, ignoring how she gasped and dug her fingers into his wet shoulders when he brushed against her clit.

"Hal, please," she said when his fingers rubbed over her entrance.

"Soon," he said before crouching and washing her legs.

"There's a bench you could sit on," she gasped when he trailed his fingers over the back of her knees.

"True," he said as he stood and grabbed the handheld and rinsed the soap from her body. "But if I sit on that bench, you'll be in my lap with my dick in your pussy."

"I don't have a problem with that," she said.

He laughed and handed her the soap. "Your turn to help me."

She bit her bottom lip, staring at the bench with real longing before soaping her hands. Anxious to fuck him, she made her movements brisk, washing his upper body and arms with quick, efficient movements.

But the low sound of Hal's moan when she gripped his erect dick with her wet soapy hand slowed her down. He slipped his arm around her waist, holding her tight as she gripped him in her hand and stroked him back and forth.

"Fuck, that feels good," he muttered.

She smiled and released him to cup his balls, gently massaging and cleaning them as Hal made another low groan. He pushed away from her and rinsed himself clean under the shower head before reaching for her.

She backed away until she bumped against the bench, grinning cheekily at him. "I haven't washed your legs yet."

"Savina," he growled. "I need to fuck you."

"Hmm," she said as she lathered her hands and sat down on the bench. "Come here."

He stood in front of her, and ignoring the beautiful sight of his very erect cock directly in front of her face, she washed his thick thighs before bending to wash his calves.

When she straightened, Hal had his cock in his hand, and he reached for her head. He cupped the back of her skull, brushing the head of his cock against her lips. "Open, sweet Savina."

She opened, and he slid his cock into her mouth, moaning her name when she immediately hollowed her cheeks around him and sucked hard. His fingers threaded through her wet hair, pulling it away from her face as he stared down at her with a glittering hot look.

"Take more," he demanded, tugging lightly on her hair.

She opened wider, taking more of him until her lips were stretched wide, and she could feel him against the back of her throat.

"Good, sweet Savina," he praised. "Keep your mouth open for me."

She did what he asked, gripping his soapy thighs as he fucked her mouth with deep thrusts that sent unexpected waves of desire washing over her. The air was hot and steamy, the shower filled with her muffled moans and Hal's low groans of pleasure.

His cock swelled in her mouth, and she suctioned around him, eager to taste his seed. He groaned and pulled out of her mouth with a low pop, shaking his head when she tried to take him back into her mouth.

"Stand up," he said.

She stood, surprised at how shaky her legs were and how much her pelvis ached. Hal rinsed his legs and then took her place on the bench, taking her hands and pulling her between his legs. He reached for her pussy, gliding his fingers through her slick wetness and smiling with satisfaction when he withdrew his fingers, and they were covered in her cream.

"Good girl, my love." He patted his lap. "Straddle me."

She climbed into his lap eagerly, appreciating how he helped steady her as her knees rested on the wet bench.

His cock was already pushing against her entrance, and he shifted her slightly, both of them crying out when her pussy sank onto his cock. She settled on his lap, gripping his shoulders tightly as he held her wet hips.

His hard thrusts rocked her on his lap, and she clung to him, moaning happily when he cupped one breast and bent his head. He sucked her tight nipple into his mouth, laving it with his tongue until the aching fierce need inside of her could no longer be contained.

She bounced on his lap, sliding up and down his hard cock as he braced his body against the slick tile and stared up at her. "You're so fucking beautiful, Savina."

"You too," she gasped, her fingers digging into his skin when he drove hard into her willing body. "Oh God, Hal…"

"Rub your clit," he ordered.

She reached down and circled her clit with her fingers. Hal watched hungrily, his hips pumping back and forth as hot steam surrounded them.

"I need you to come, love." A look of sudden desperation crossed Hal's face as he moved faster inside of her. "Can you be my good girl and come on my cock?"

Hot desire slammed into her, and she rubbed furiously at her clit, as Hal bellowed a curse before his body stiffened, and he thrust hard into her. Hot liquid filled her pussy, and she cried out, her climax hitting her in an exhilarating rush of pleasure.

She slumped against him, their bodies shaking as they rode out the last of their orgasms together. Hal rubbed her wet back with long lazy strokes, his warm breath puffing in her ear.

She kissed his neck. "That was amazing. Thank you."

"My pleasure, sweet Savina."

She eased off of him, and they stood under the showerheads, both doing a quick clean-up before the hot water tank could run completely dry.

They climbed out of the shower and wrapped towels around themselves before staring a little self-consciously at each other. After a moment, Hal said, "I should probably go."

His stomach growled, and Savina held out her hand. "I promised you a delicious dinner of sandwiches, remember?"

He smiled, took her hand, and let her lead him into the bedroom. She opened her closet and scanned the clothes. "You can put your clothes in the wash while we eat dinner, so you don't have to smell puppy poop while you're eating. But the only thing I have that might fit you is this." She held out her silky peach robe, smiling when Hal took it without hesitating.

He put it on, tying the sash closed before grinning at her. "How does it look?"

"Peach definitely works with your skin tone," she said.

He laughed, and she quickly dressed in a cotton pajama set with neon pink flamingos.

"Cute," he said. "I like the flamingos."

"Thank you," she said. "Ready for the best sandwich you've ever had?"

"Ready," he said and, after a moment's hesitation, took her hand and followed her out of the room.

"ARE YOU SURE YOU DON'T WANT ANOTHER SANDWICH?" Savina asked.

Hal loaded the last plate into the dishwasher. "Positive."

She nodded but still looked unconvinced. "I have some veggies and hummus in the fridge if you're still hungry.

We used a lot of energy today, and a sandwich isn't a big dinner."

"I'm full, I swear." Hal checked the time on the microwave. It was close to ten, and he knew Savina wasn't a night owl. So, why wasn't he grabbing his clothes from the dryer? Why wasn't he saying goodnight and going home to his apartment?

You know why. You don't want to leave her. Ever.

Could you blame him? Her shower was magnificent, and she had puppies to cuddle. No one would want to leave.

You're fucking fooling yourself if you don't realize the only reason you want to stay is because you're in love with Savina.

Guilt and a heavy dose of sorrow made him droop against the counter. It should have been Alan here with Savina, not him. He didn't deserve this. He didn't deserve her, and he never would. Not after how he'd felt or the shit he'd thought.

"Hal?" Savina's cool hands cupped his face. "Honey, are you okay?"

"Fine," he said hoarsely. "It's getting late. I'd better go."

"I'd like you to stay the night," she said, and the vulnerability in her voice stopped his protest before it even formed.

"Are you sure?" he rasped.

She nodded, her thumbs brushing over his cheekbones. "If you're comfortable with that."

He nodded, and she pressed a gentle kiss against his mouth before stepping back. Savina let Izzie into the backyard before putting her in the dining room with the babies and closing the door.

He took her hand, and she linked their fingers together as they climbed the stairs to her room. He hesitated when he saw the bed, and her voice soft, Savina said, "It's a new bed. I bought it three months ago, but I'll understand if you don't want to sleep in here. We can sleep in the guest room if you prefer."

"I'm good with it but are you sure you are?" he asked.

She nodded, turning on the bedside lamp and studying the room. "I loved this room when it was mine and Alan's, but I've made a lot of changes since he died. New flooring, new paint," she brushed her hand over the bed, "a new bed with all new bedding. It feels like just my room now, and I think that's how it should be."

She stepped closer to him, her face a soft shadow in the dim light. "While I will always love Alan, he's gone, and he isn't coming back. He'd approve of me working through my grief by donating most of his stuff, changing things at the house, and being with you. He wouldn't want me to wallow in the grief, just like Mary wouldn't want you to, either."

"I know," he said, but the guilt still crept around his edges, poking and prodding and making his skin feel too thin and jagged.

She cupped his face, staring intently at him. "Do you?"

"Yes," he said.

She continued to study him until growing uncomfortable by what he suspected was her ability to tell when he was bullshitting her, he stepped back and said, "Do you have an extra toothbrush I can use?"

"Yes," she said, her face still hidden in the shadows.

They went into the bathroom, and she found him a new toothbrush. They stood at the double vanity. Hal brushed his teeth as Savina did the same before smoothing on some cream on her face and a clear liquid that she told him was 'magic in a bottle'. There was a weird type of comfort in sharing the before bedtime routine with Savina that he tried not to read too much into. As amazing as this was, it wouldn't work out long term with her. His guilt would never allow it.

Then get your ass back to therapy and work through the guilt!

"Hal? Do you prefer the left or right side?" Savina called from the bedroom.

He joined her by the bed. "I usually sleep on the right, but I can switch it up."

"I sleep on the left," she said with a small smile. She pulled back the quilt and sheet, and Hal took off his robe before they slid into the bed. The coolness of the sheets gave him goosebumps.

Savina plugged in her phone, set her alarm, and shut the light off before snuggling close to him. "I love my house, but I hate how cold this room gets in the winter."

He wrapped his arms around her, staring at how her silky hair draped across his skin as she rested her cheek on his chest. He rubbed her back, listening to the house creak and groan as it settled for the night, and the sound of Savina's soft and even breathing.

He'd assumed Savina invited him to spend the night only because she wanted sex again. But while she brushed her hand up and down his ribcage, it conveyed comfort more than need.

Unexpected warmth rushed through him. Not that he

expected Savina to feel anything for him more than lust, but lying here in Savina's bed with her soft warmth pressed up against him repaired the cracks in his heart in a way he'd never thought possible.

Tomorrow they would return to being friends, and he'd never have this with her again, but tonight... tonight, he would enjoy every moment.

CHAPTER 13

"Whoa, girl. Steady, Penny." Hal rubbed the horse's thick neck as Nathan paused in suturing the small gash on her flank.

"You sure you don't want to put her in the stocks, Doc?" Solomon asked.

"We're good. It won't be much longer." Nathan paused in his suturing of Penny's flank as Hal took a firmer grip on her halter. "You good, Hal?"

"Yes," Hal said as Solomon leaned against the stall wall and stared at his phone.

"Any idea how she did this?" Hal asked.

Solomon tucked his phone into his pocket. "Not a damn clue. Wyatt saw blood in the paddock and followed the trail straight to Penny. How's it look, Doc?"

"It's small but pretty deep," Nathan said. He continued to suture as Solomon joined him and squinted at the gash.

"Christ, that's some fine stitchwork," Solomon said.

Nathan laughed. "Thank you. Hey, how's your barn cat doing? The one Heather brought in the other day?"

"He's good. No longer limping, and the swelling is completely gone from his leg. Although it's hell giving him his antibiotics. He's one of my best mousers, but Christ, he's a miserable son of a bitch."

Nathan laughed again as Hal said, "You should have seen me trying to hold him for Nathan's exam. I still hear his screaming in my dreams."

"The cat or the doc?" Solomon asked with a grin.

"Definitely mine," Nathan said as he made the final stitch and cut the suture material. He drew up the antibiotics into a syringe and administered it. "I'll get Hal to dispense some oral antibiotics as well. It should keep any infection at bay but call the clinic if she shows redness or swelling around the wound."

"Will do. I'll get Wyatt to separate her from the others for a few days. Penny's one of his favourites. He'll keep a close eye on her," Solomon said.

Hal stroked Penny's neck again as Nathan gave her the shot and then stripped off his gloves. "Okay, that should do it. I'll put in a recheck call in two days."

His phone rang, and he pulled it from his pocket. "It's the clinic. Excuse me."

He grabbed his bag and left the stall, walking to the far end of the barn. Hal let go of Penny's halter, gave her one final pat and followed Solomon out of the stall. Solomon secured the stall before leaning against it and giving him an assessing look.

"What?" Hal asked.

"You look like shit."

"It's been a long week," Hal said.

"You finished work for the day?" Solomon asked.

Hal nodded. "Yeah, this was our last appointment." He

had followed Nathan on his bike so he could head straight home rather than return to the clinic.

"Stay for supper," Solomon said.

"You have enough mouths to feed," Hal said. "You don't need one extra."

"Shit, man, you know Heather always makes enough food to feed an army. There will be plenty, even with those ravenous boys I call ranch hands."

Hal laughed. "You hire a bunch of twenty-something-year-olds, and of course they're gonna eat you out of house and home."

Solomon shrugged. "Don't I know it. So, you staying or not? It might be a Friday night, but I fucking know you don't have any plans. You never have plans."

"Because I work tomorrow," Hal said.

"Uh-huh. You're staying for supper."

"I appreciate the offer, but I'm exhausted, and I just want to go home," Hal said.

"Your mood have anything to do with Savina?" Solomon asked.

Hal jerked before checking to see where Nathan was. He was still at the far end of the barn, listening intently to the person on the other end of the phone.

"No, why?"

"Well, ain't that some bullshit. Heather had coffee with Savina yesterday morning and said Savina looks just as mopey as you do. Did you two fight?"

"No," Hal said. "We're friends again."

"Is that right?" Solomon said.

Hal nodded, looking away from his best friend's steady gaze. Just because Hal had turned down both of Savina's requests to have dinner this week didn't mean they weren't friends. It just meant he was swamped, that's all.

He scrubbed a hand through his hair. He hadn't seen Savina since Sunday afternoon when they'd finished helping Warren unpack the U-Haul at his condo. His temptation to go back home with Savina afterward, despite his aching muscles and exhaustion, had been tough to ignore. But Savina had made no indication earlier that morning at her place that she wanted him anymore. She'd already been up and showered by the time he dragged his tired ass out of her much too comfortable bed a full hour after he normally woke. She'd made him breakfast and been her usual, cheerful self, but she hadn't touched or looked at him in any way that suggested she might want another go at his dick.

He nudged a rock with his foot, continuing to avoid Solomon's razor sharp gaze. Savina had satisfied her itch for him, and he had to learn to be okay with that. He'd had two nights with her, one more night than he'd expected, and he needed to stop sulking like a big-ass baby.

But we didn't even get to taste her pussy.

No, he hadn't, and not going down on Savina once they'd gone to bed on Saturday night would forever be one of the biggest fucking regrets of his life.

"Hey, come back to me, asshole." Solomon gave him a friendly poke in the shoulder. "What's going on with you and Savina?"

"Nothing," Hal said in a low voice as Nathan walked toward them. "Just drop it, Solomon."

"That was Jade at the clinic," Nathan said. "A dog came in that got tore up in a fight. I need to head back."

"I can come back and assist," Hal said.

Nathan shook his head, staring distractedly at his phone. "No, that's okay. Jade said she could stay. But I told Savina Ras I would drop off the dewormer for the puppies on the way back to the clinic. Do you think you could drop it off for me?"

Hal plastered a smile on his face. "Sure, that's no problem."

"Great. I'll grab the dewormer from my truck," Nathan said.

"I'll talk to you later," Hal said to Solomon.

Solomon nodded. "We're gonna talk soon, Hal. Real soon."

His stomach knotted up tight, Hal followed Nathan out of the barn.

"HAL! HI!" THE HAPPINESS ON SAVINA'S FACE WHEN SHE opened the door made Hal feel good.

It made him feel like a fucking rockstar, if he was being honest.

"Hi," he said.

"How are you?" Savina asked, then looked down at his motorcycle boots. "Shit, sorry, come inside. It's freezing out today. Did you ride here?"

"I did." He stepped inside the warm house, trying not to notice how fucking cute she looked with her hair up in a messy bun and wearing pink plaid pajama bottoms and an oversized sweatshirt with a peeling graphic of David Bowie on the front. Christ, he was almost certain she wasn't wearing a bra.

"You must be freezing. Come to the kitchen, and I'll get you some tea," Savina said.

He hung his jacket on the coat tree and took off his boots before following Savina. He sat at the table, placing the bag with the dewormer on it, and she made them both tea before sliding into the seat next to his. "How was work today?"

"Good, thanks." He pointed to the bag. "Here's the dewormer for the puppies. Nathan had an emergency at the clinic and asked me to drop it off after we finished at Solomon's."

Savina stared at the paper bag, the happiness on her face dissolving like sugar in the rain. "You're here to drop off dewormer."

"Yes," he said. "What's wrong?"

"What's wrong?" She glared at him before shoving to her feet. She grabbed her mug and his and stomped to the sink, dumping the hot liquid down the drain before turning to him. "You seriously don't know what's wrong, Hal?"

"I know you're angry with me," he said.

She snorted, crossing her arms over her chest and scowling. "Damn right I am. You've been avoiding me since Sunday even though you promised - *promised* - we would be friends again. Then you finally show up on my doorstep, and it's to deliver stupid dewormer!"

"Savina, I -"

"Leave," she snapped. "You're being a complete asshole, and I don't want to spend another minute with you."

He walked toward her, his steps slowing at the look on her face. Shit, this wasn't just Savina's short temper getting the best of her. This was pure fury aimed directly at him.

"You're right," he said, employing the voice he used to soothe angry cats. "I'm being an asshole."

"Don't you dare use your 'calm down, you crazy cat' voice on me, Hal McGinnis!"

Savina was nearly spitting with rage, and he'd never found her more fucking beautiful.

"I shouldn't have avoided you and -"

"No, you shouldn't have!" she said. "We're both too old to be playing these fucking games. If you just wanted to get laid and not be friends, you should have just said that, Hal."

"That isn't what I want," he said.

"Oh really?" She stalked forward until her folded arms brushed against his chest. "Because that's exactly what it looks like."

"I know, but…"

Christ, she was so gorgeous. And now that he was closer to her, he could see the damp tendrils of hair that had escaped her bun and curled against her neck. He could smell the vanilla scent of her body wash and see the faint hint of her nipples against the sweatshirt.

Lust nearly knocked him off his feet. He took a deep breath, trying to focus on Savina and her anger with him. He might want to fuck her silly right now, but that was the last thing on her mind. He'd be lucky if she didn't boot him in the ass as she walked him out the front door.

"But what?" she said. "Do you know how hurtful it was to have you blow me off this week, Hal? I get it, okay? You don't want to be friends, and -"

"I want to be friends!" Now his voice was too loud. "I want to be friends, Savina, but I can't."

"Why?" she asked.

Thrown off by her straightforwardness, he said, "Because I want to fuck you. Every goddamn time I'm with you."

She blinked at him, and he would have laughed at the shock on her face if he wasn't feeling so damn terrible. He'd lost Savina as a lover, and now he'd lost her as a friend, and how miserable of an existence would he live knowing that he could never have what he wanted most.

"I have to go," he said. He couldn't stand here in her kitchen a minute fucking longer. Couldn't smell her sweet scent or stare at her gorgeous face knowing she'd never be his.

He grunted in surprise when Savina nearly threw herself at him. He caught her automatically, his hands sliding around her waist as she slammed her mouth down on his and kissed him with a desperate need that skyrocketed his own.

He cupped the back of her head, sliding his tongue into her mouth and groaning harshly when she sucked on his tongue. They kissed until they ran out of air and were forced to break apart. He stared silently at her before grabbing her sweatshirt and yanking it over her head.

Her squeak of surprise turned into a moan when he cupped her naked breasts and bent his head, sucking on each nipple until they turned to hard buds in his mouth. She clutched at his head, arching her back and pulling his hair as he worshipped her perfect breasts with his lips and tongue.

She didn't object when he turned her and backed her

toward the big farmhouse table that dominated the kitchen. He lifted her and set her on the table, pushing her onto her back before grabbing her pajama bottoms.

"Lift your hips," he said.

She lifted them, and he pulled down her pajamas, the air exiting his lungs in an exquisite rush when he saw her naked core.

"No panties?" he said as he dropped her pants on the floor before pulling his shirt over his head and tossing it onto a chair.

"I just got out of the bath," she said.

"Your skin is so fucking soft." He stroked the front of her thighs before sliding his hands between them and pushing. "Open for me."

She let her legs drop open, and he studied her pussy before trailing one finger through the short patch of hair at the top. "So beautiful, sweet Savina."

"Thank you." Her voice was unsteady, and she gasped when he rubbed her clit.

He bent and pressed a kiss against the curve of her stomach before kissing his way down one smooth thigh. When he licked the soft skin of her inner thigh, she moaned, and her hips rose in a silent plea.

He grinned to himself and kissed her other thigh, licking and nibbling at her skin until her hand gripped his short hair. She pulled hard, and he lifted his head to smile at her. "Yes, love?"

"I want more," she said.

"Is that right?" He kissed the top of her pussy, and Savina made a small sound of disappointment when he moved to her hip and nibbled it.

"Hal!"

"Ask me nicely," he said.

She glared at him, and he ran his fingers up and down her inner thighs. "Ask me nicely to eat your sweet pussy, and I will."

She moaned when he used his shoulders to spread her legs wider and licked the crease between her pussy and thigh. "Not until you ask me, Savina."

"Oh God," she breathed out. "Please eat my pussy, Hal."

"Good girl," he murmured and licked up her slit from her opening to her clit. She cried out, her hips bucking wildly, and he pinned her to the table with his hands on her hips. She tasted so fucking good, like the sweetest honey, and he licked her again before concentrating on her pink clit. He sucked and licked at it, teasing it with slow strokes of his tongue until it was visible between her wet pussy lips.

He took another long lick of her cream, groaning at her sweet taste as she moaned his name and gripped his head. She tried to push him back to her clit, and he went willingly, sucking on her clit again as he slid two fingers into her tight entrance. She squeezed around his fingers, and the tight wetness was almost his undoing. He wanted, *needed*, to be in her.

He sucked hard on her clit, fucking her roughly with his fingers as Savina's cries turned loud and frantic. Her hips bucked once, twice, and then her body stiffened, and sweet liquid coated his mouth. She shook against his mouth, moaning his name in a low litany as he licked her clean before straightening.

"Oh my God," she gasped out. "That was, I mean... that was everything I'd ever fantasized it would be."

He grinned as he scooped his shirt up and used it to wipe his short beard. "This was a fantasy for you?"

"Hell, yes." She sat up and pressed a kiss against his mouth. "Thank you."

"You're welcome. Stand up for me."

She stood, giggling when she was a little wobbly and gave him a questioning look over her shoulder when he turned her around to face the table. "Hal?"

"Your turn to fulfill my fantasy," he said as he unbuttoned his jeans and shoved them and his briefs down to his ankles. "Bend over, love."

She hesitated, and he pressed hard on her upper back, forcing her down to the table as he pushed her legs apart with one thigh. He lined his cock up to her glistening entrance, keeping her pinned to the table with one hand while he gripped a handful of her firm ass with the other.

"Hal, I -"

He pushed into her with one smooth motion, enjoying the sound of her soft gasp and how she gripped the sides of the table. He watched her pussy lips spread around his dick, squeezing her ass tighter when she wiggled against him.

"No, Savina. Stay still for me."

"Hal, it's too much," she moaned.

"I know, my love," he said but kept pushing forward.

"Oh, God." She wiggled and squirmed, her hands squeezing the sides of the table as he pushed forward until he was fully seated inside her. He lifted his hand from her back, smiling his approval when she didn't straighten. He rubbed her ass, kneading and lightly stroking as he waited for her to relax.

"You're so pretty stuffed full of my dick," he said and

rubbed her lower back. Stay just like this while I fuck you, Savina."

"Yes, Hal."

Fresh lust washed over him, and he gripped her hips tight before pounding into her. He wanted to go slow, should have gone slow, but those two soft words from her perfect lips had ignited a fire in him that he couldn't contain.

He slammed in and out of her, the smooth slick grip of her pussy making his entire body shudder with pleasure. His orgasm hovered right on the surface, and as much as he wanted to make this moment last, wanted to keep living out his very detailed fantasy of fucking Savina over her kitchen table, he was helpless to deny its insistent call. He clamped a hand down on Savina's shoulder with his other hand still wrapped around her hip and thrust hard. Savina cried out, her perfect ass bouncing under his hard thrusts, her fingers gripping the table until they turned white.

"So fucking beautiful," he moaned before making one final deep thrust. He held Savina tight as he came deep into her pussy, his body shuddering and shaking before he collapsed against her back.

"Oof," Savina said, her voice muffled. "Hal, you're squishing me."

He straightened, staggering a little on his feet when he eased out of her, his dick coated in her sweet cream. He helped her straighten, and she turned around, leaning against the table as she stared at him.

"Are you okay?" he rasped. Now that his need for Savina had been satisfied, he was a little ashamed at how rough he'd been with her and how he'd gone after his climax without a single thought of giving her a second one.

"Yes," she said. "It was… unexpected, but also the hottest fuck of my life."

"I should have made you come again," he said.

She smiled, reaching out to trail her fingers through his chest hair. "Yes, you should have. So, what do you say we get into my amazing shower, and you give me that second one, handsome?"

He grinned at her. "Whatever you want, pretty lady."

CHAPTER 14

"Hal, seriously, you don't have to keep helping me clean the puppy pen." Savina laid down the final pee pad in the nursery pen before stepping over the wooden wall.

Hal tied the garbage bag closed as the puppies circled him like furry sharks before the biggest one pounced on him and bit his leg through his jeans.

"Ouch!" Hal pulled the puppy off of his leg. "No biting, buddy."

He set the puppy down, and it scampered off to join its siblings, who had raced across the room to nip at Izzie's legs.

"I'll take this out to the garbage can." Hal picked up the garbage bag and left the dining room.

Savina popped the puppies back into the pen, giving each one a snuggle as Izzie jumped into the pen and relaxed on her side. The puppies crowded up to the milk bar, two of them jostling for a nipple before the smaller one gave up and latched onto a different one.

Savina stroked Izzie's head. "You're a good mama, Izzie."

She left the babies to eat their dinner and went to the kitchen, washing her hands and smiling at Hal when he came in through the back door. She patted his chest as he walked by her to wash his hands. "You should have thrown your jacket on. It's cold tonight."

"It is," he said.

"Does it look like it's going to snow?" she asked.

Hal rinsed the soap off his hands and dried them on a tea towel. "No, it's a clear night."

She hoped her disappointment didn't show. It was the perfect excuse to keep Hal with her for the night if it was snowing or going to snow. He couldn't ride his bike in the snow, right? That was just basic bike safety.

Her stomach growled, and Hal glanced at his watch. "I should probably go so you can eat dinner."

"Or, you can stay and eat dinner with me," she said. "I'm making a fast and simple stir fry. Won't take more than half an hour."

"Thank you for the dinner invite," he said.

"But?"

"But nothing," he said with a small grin. "I love stir fry."

She laughed and opened the fridge to grab the vegetables. "Can you chop some veggies for me while I get the chicken started?"

"Sure," he said.

They worked in comfortable silence, and she tried not to read too much into the moment. Of course they would work well together. They'd been best friends for nearly two years, and it was easy to fall back into the rhythm of their natural compatibility.

And being with him is even better now that you know how good he is at fucking.

Wasn't that the truth. She dropped the chicken pieces into the wok, and the oil sizzled and popped. She added some spices and stirred as Hal brought the vegetables to her.

"Thank you," she said.

"You bet. I checked the latch on the ladies' house when I was in the backyard, so you don't need to do your bedtime check."

"You remembered that I do a second check," she said. Warmth washed over her, and while it was a little foolish to be so happy that Hal knew her routine with her chickens, she couldn't help it. She loved that he knew her so well.

He rinsed off the cutting board and loaded it into the dishwasher. "Thank you for inviting me to stay for dinner."

She decided to go for it. "I'd like you to stay the night as well. I know you work in the morning, but I'm happy to set the alarm earlier."

She poked at the cooking chicken, telling herself not to be upset when Hal said no.

The silence stretched out, and she glanced at him. "There's no pressure to say yes."

"I want to say yes," Hal said, leaning a hip against the counter. "But I also don't want to give you the wrong idea or…."

He trailed off before rubbing a hand against his beard. "Shit, I'm fucking this up already."

"No, you're not." She stirred the veggies and the chicken so she wouldn't have to look straight at him. He'd see the lie on her face if she did. "I know this would be a friends with benefits type thing, and I'm good with that."

"Are you?" Hal asked.

She pulled out her rusty skills from her grade ten 'I want to be an actor' stage and pasted on a convincing smile before turning to face him. "Positive. I'm not ready for a new relationship at this point."

That was one whopper of a lie, but she'd rather have a friends with benefits with Hal than nothing at all. And it was obvious to them both that they couldn't return to being just friends. At least not until they'd fucked away whatever this was between them.

You really think that's possible?

Maybe, maybe not. But it didn't matter, did it? Hal didn't want more, and she wouldn't push him for it. She'd take what he was offering until it was no longer enough for her, and then she'd gather up her dignity and the pieces of her shattered heart and accept that Hal couldn't give her what she needed.

———

"YOU LOOK DIFFERENT." WANDA EYED SAVINA ACROSS the small table they'd snagged at Grind My Beans.

Savina sipped at her coffee. Grind My Beans was swamped with people, not surprising for a Saturday afternoon, and she leaned forward so she didn't have to yell. "What do you mean?"

"You look happier," Wanda said.

Savina shrugged. "I feel the same."

She took another sip of coffee, hoping Wanda wouldn't see through her lie. She *was* happier. Much happier, in fact, and it had everything to do with Hal. It'd only been a week since they decided to be friends with benefits, but Hal had spent every night at her place. Last Monday, on Hal's day off, they'd taken advantage of the nice weather to take a bike ride down to Riverton. They ate lunch at a cute little restaurant overlooking the bay and did some antique shopping at a few different shops. While they hadn't held hands or done anything that suggested they were dating, Savina had been a little embarrassed by how giddily happy it made her to be with him.

Wanda still studied her, and Savina hurried to change the subject. "How was the meeting this week?"

"Good, cathartic for more than one of us. I thought you were planning on being there?" Wanda said.

"Oh, I ended up with other plans," Savina said.

"Is that right?"

"Mm, hmm. So, what do you have planned for tonight?" Savina asked.

"Nothing as exciting as you," Wanda said.

Savina cleared her throat. "What do you mean?"

"I mean, you have the look of a woman who's getting it on the regular. Who's your new guy?" Wanda said with a grin.

Savina blushed. "Um, he's not, I mean… we're not… it's Hal."

To her credit, Wanda's eyebrows only raised a little. "So, your plan worked then?"

"It did," Savina said. "We're friends again."

"But not just friends."

"Well, we had sex once with the understanding that after, we would only be friends, but...."

"But you kept wanting to see each other naked?" Wanda said.

Savina laughed. "That's an accurate description."

"Well, I'm delighted that you and Hal are dating," Wanda said before taking a delicate bite of her pastry.

"Oh, uh, we're not dating," Savina said. "It's a friends with benefits thing."

"Why?" Wanda asked bluntly.

"That's all Hal wants," Savina said.

"So, you get together once or twice a week?" Wanda asked.

"We haven't really talked about that," Savina said. "We decided last weekend to be friends with benefits, and Hal's come by after work every night this week, and he stays over at my place."

"Every night?" This time Wanda's eyebrows nearly disappeared into her hairline. "That doesn't sound like a friends with benefits to me."

"I wasn't expecting him to stay at my house every night," Savina admitted, "but I like that he is. I like it a lot."

"You want more, don't you?" Wanda said.

Savina nodded. "Yes."

"Have you told Hal that you want more?"

"I haven't."

Wanda smiled at her. "From my perspective, it seems like Hal might want more too. Why don't you talk with him about it?"

"I guess I'm afraid it'll push him away," Savina said. "I want more, but I also don't want to lose what we have.

I've missed him so much this last year and to be friends again with the bonus of sleeping with him is amazing."

"I get being afraid of losing him again, but you know better than anyone how short and precious life can be. Going after what you want, being with the person you love, is important, right?" Wanda said.

"I'm not in love with Hal," Savina said.

"Aren't you?"

She stared at Wanda before sitting back in her chair. "Shit. I'm in love with Hal."

Wanda laughed. "Girl, it's about time you caught up to the rest of the class. You even say that boy's name, and hearts drip from your eyes."

"Okay, so I'm in love with Hal, which means if he rejects me, it's even worse. Now I've lost the man I love and my best friend. I think it's better just to accept what he's offering."

"That's your fear talking," Wanda said. "I know the prospect of losing Hal is hard, but you won't be happy long term with this arrangement, and then what? You stay even though you're miserable? That's not good for you or Hal."

Savina took a deep breath. The coffee in her stomach suddenly felt a little like battery acid, and even the thought of talking to Hal made her tense, but what Wanda said was true. She wanted more from Hal, and it wasn't fair to either of them for her to pretend she didn't.

"If he rejects me, it'll be, well... it'll be devastating," Savina said.

"It's hard to put yourself out there, to be vulnerable even with the people you love," Wanda said. "But do you really think Hal will reject you?"

Savina took another drink of coffee as she thought over Wanda's question. She may have been new to the world of friends with benefits, but Hal's actions this week suggested he wanted more. What if he was holding back because he thought that was what she wanted? What if she told him how she felt, and that's all he'd been waiting to hear?

She smiled at Wanda as excitement replaced the worry in her belly. "No, I don't think he will. I think, I *hope*, that Hal wants more, but I won't know unless I tell him how I feel and ask him if he feels the same, right?"

"That's right," Wanda said.

Savina sat back in her chair. "I'm going to talk to him. Thank you, Wanda."

Wanda reached out and squeezed her hand. "You deserve every happiness in the world, Savina."

CHAPTER 15

"You're a good girl, Izzie." Hal rubbed Izzie's ears as she leaned against his legs. He put the lid on the garbage can and walked back into Savina's house. Izzie followed him inside and went straight to the dining room, hopping into the freshly-cleaned puppy pen. The puppies started a chorus of cries that ended when Izzie laid down to nurse them.

Hal returned to the kitchen. He finished setting the table, smiling when he heard Savina's truck in the driveway. He opened the bottle of wine as she entered the front door in a gust of cold air.

"Hal?"

"Hey, I'm in the kitchen." He poured wine into two glasses and turned to face her as she walked through the doorway.

"Oh my God, it smells so good in here." She grinned at him as she shrugged off her jacket and laid it over one of the extra kitchen chairs.

"I hope you don't mind that I used my key to let

myself in." Alan had given him a key years ago, and he'd never gotten around to returning it. He handed her the wine glass, and she took a sip.

After leaving the clinic, he'd picked up a bottle of her favourite Chardonnay, and he loved the delighted smile that crossed her face as she tasted it.

"My favourite," she said. "And you know I don't mind at all. Mi casa es su casa."

He pointed to her chair. "Have a seat while I serve up dinner."

She sat in the chair. "I should be the one making you dinner. I didn't work all day."

He shrugged as he took the coleslaw from the fridge and spooned it into two salad bowls. "You know I like to cook."

"I know, but I'm sure you're tired."

"I'm good." He used oven mitts to pull out the stuffed chicken breasts and the crispy potato wedges, placing both baking trays on the stovetop.

He grinned when he felt Savina's soft warmth against his back as she peeked over his shoulder. "Oh my God! Did you make mushroom stuffed chicken breasts and potato wedges?"

"I did," he said.

She turned him around and draped her arms over his shoulders, pressing an enthusiastic kiss against his mouth. "My favourite wine and favourite meal. What's the occasion?"

"No occasion, just felt like doing something nice for you," he said.

Her radiant smile healed another section of his cracked heart. "It's a wonderful surprise, and I love it. Thank you."

"You're welcome." He kissed her again, letting his mouth linger on hers until she pressed herself against his growing erection and made those soft, intoxicating moans he'd grown to crave.

She pulled back, giving him a cute grin. "We need to stop before I take you to the bedroom, and this delicious food gets cold."

"You have a microwave," he said before palming her ass.

"Tempting, but you shouldn't have made my favourite food. My growling stomach demands satisfaction."

He laughed and gave her a gentle push back toward the table. "Fair enough."

He went to work dishing out the food onto the plates as Savina disappeared into the dining room. She came back a few minutes later. "Hal, you cleaned the puppy pen?"

"I did," he said. "I needed something to do while the food was cooking."

"Oh my God, you might be the perfect man." She sat down and took another sip of wine.

"Not even close," he said as he set the bowls of coleslaw on the table before bringing over the plates. He set them down and sat in the chair next to hers. Savina stared at the food, and he could almost see her mouth watering.

"This looks and smells delicious."

"Dig in," he said.

They ate silently, Savina making cute little sounds of happiness as she sampled everything. "This is perfection. Seriously, Hal."

"I'm glad you're enjoying it. How was your day?" He ate a bite of chicken before swallowing some wine.

"It was nice. I had a few people stop by for egg pickups this morning, and then I had coffee with Wanda and stopped at Warren's new place after that. I helped him do more unpacking and hang some pictures. It's why I'm a bit late. How was your day?"

"Good. Busy at the clinic, but not insane." He ate a forkful of coleslaw and then a potato wedge, raising his eyebrows when he realized that Savina had stopped eating and was staring at him. "You okay?"

"I am," she said. "I wanted to talk to you about something."

"Okay," he said.

She hesitated, studying him and the food on the table before she shook her head. "You know what? Never mind. We can talk about it another time."

"Are you sure?" he asked.

"Positive." She gave him another bright and beaming smile. "Are you staying the night?"

"Yes, if you're okay with that?"

"Of course," she said. "There's a new HBO show I want to watch. I thought we could start it tonight."

"Sure." They lapsed into a comfortable silence as they ate. The nagging worry that she might not want him to stay the night was gone, and he dug into the food with a renewed relish. He'd spent every night this week with her and while he knew it was too much, knew that his actions came across as more than a friends with benefits relationship, he couldn't help himself. Being with Savina felt as necessary as breathing to him.

You should slow down. Spending every night with her, making her favourite dinner... you're sending all the wrong signals, buddy.

He ignored his inner voice. He and Savina were friends, and friends did nice things for each other.

"You okay?" Savina touched his hand, and he turned it over so he could link their fingers together.

He pushed away the lingering doubt. "I'm good."

"ESTHER, STOP THAT! LOUANNE, DON'T BE SO PUSHY. There's plenty for everyone." Savina added the last of the greens to the pans she'd set up as the chickens jostled for a place at each pan.

She moved Louanne away from Esther, the two hens were always quick to fight, and added more feed to the long feeder tray while the girls gobbled up the greens. She collected the eggs and added them to the basket before stepping out of the coop and into the large covered mesh run attached to the coop. Her worry that foxes or coyotes would break into the mesh run and attack her girls had never come to fruition, thanks to the combined efforts of Alan, Hal, and Solomon. They'd spent a weekend building the secure and sturdy mesh run when she'd first decided to start her egg business.

Ruth and Bonnie had followed her out into the run, and she spent a few moments petting each hen and giving them some love before picking up her basket of eggs and heading toward the house.

The sun had risen, but the air was cold, and she walked briskly. Hal was still sleeping when she climbed out of bed, showered, and dressed quietly. They'd stayed up too late last night. After watching nearly four episodes of the HBO show, it had been close to midnight before they'd crawled into bed. Despite neither being night owls, the late hour hadn't stopped them from having sex. She couldn't get enough of Hal's body, his touch, or how he made her feel. It was the sweetest addiction, one she didn't want to kick.

She had meant to talk to Hal last night about how she felt but, in the end, decided not to. Hal had gone to a lot of work to make her favourite dinner, and she hadn't wanted to potentially ruin the moment by forcing him to talk about his feelings for her. She had plenty of time to talk to him. In fact, she would speak to him this morning. She wanted Hal to know how she truly felt about him, even if he didn't feel the same way.

But deep down, you're confident he loves you, aren't you?

Yes, she was. Maybe that made her arrogant, but she wasn't some young girl who didn't know what love was. How Hal looked at her and treated her... he loved her. She was sure of it.

She unlatched the back gate of the fenced-in portion of her backyard, closing it firmly behind her as Izzie looked up from where she sniffed at the patio bricks. She loped toward Savina, bumping her legs with her head until Savina stopped and petted her.

"Morning, sweetheart. Once it warms up later, we'll bring your babies out into the yard to run off some of their energy. What do you say, sweet girl?" She rubbed Izzie's throat, smiling when the dog leaned against her legs before sniffing at the egg basket.

"C'mon, Izzie, I'll make you a special treat this morning of a few scrambled eggs because you're such a good girl."

Izzie followed her into the house, and Savina washed her hands before scrambling the eggs for Izzie. As the dog ate them enthusiastically, Savina started the coffee pot. She wasn't much of a breakfast eater, but Hal was, and she idly checked the fridge. She would make him some French toast. A thank you for the delicious dinner and the three orgasms he'd given her last night.

She grabbed the bread from the cupboard, turning around when the front door slammed, and her brother called her name.

Shit!

"In the kitchen," she said. Hal had parked his bike in his usual spot against the side of the house, so unless Warren had taken a walk around the property before coming in, he wouldn't have seen it.

"Hey." Warren walked into the kitchen and helped himself to a cup of coffee before dropping into a chair. Izzie immediately crowded up to him, resting her head in his lap. "How's it going?"

"Good," she said. "What's up? You're here early."

He grinned at her. "So? You're a morning person. Can't a guy stop by his sister's house on a Sunday morning for no reason?"

She rolled her eyes. "Nice try, buddy. You want something... spill it."

He laughed and sipped at his steaming cup of coffee. "I'm heading up to the flea market over in Willington. You want to come with?"

"Oh, um, maybe."

The silence drew out as she tried to think of a plausible excuse for not going. Warren petted Izzie with one hand

and stared at her over his coffee mug, one bushy eyebrow raised questioningly.

"Thank you for the invite, but -"

"Is that coffee I smell? Pour me an extra-large cup. I need the caffeine after you kept me awake late with your insatiable demands for sex." Hal strolled into the kitchen, wearing just a pair of jeans and his hair still damp from the shower.

"Hal?" Warren set his coffee cup on the table with a thump. "What are you... I mean...?"

Hal stared wide-eyed at Warren before turning to stare at Savina. Willing herself not to blush, Savina said, "Thanks for the invite to the flea market, Warren, but I'll have to take a rain check."

Warren didn't even glance her way. She knew her brother well enough to know he wasn't angry or upset, but a thick layer of shock covered his face. "You and Savina are sleeping together?"

Hal cleared his throat, rubbing self-consciously at one forearm. "Warren, I... yes, we are."

"She's your best friend's wife," Warren said.

Hal winced, and Savina said, "I'm a widow, Warren."

Warren shook his head before staring at her. "Right, sorry. Yeah, no, I didn't mean...."

He trailed off, leaving the air thick with embarrassment and surprise.

Hal gripped the back of an empty chair. "Warren, it's not -"

"I should go." Warren stood up abruptly, pushing his chair back with a loud scrape as Izzie chuffed in surprise and backed away. "Sorry to interrupt. I shouldn't have... I mean... I'm gonna go so you two can... do whatever you were ... I'm gonna go."

He turned and strode out of the kitchen, shutting the door behind him. Savina burst into giggles, the look of discomfort on her brother's face familiar. The idea of his baby sister having sex had grossed him out from the time they were teenagers, and she found it endlessly amusing.

She turned to Hal, the giggles dying out. "Hal? Honey, are you okay?"

"I'm fine," he said.

She hurried over to him, sliding her arms around his waist. "Warren wasn't upset, honey. I know my brother, and that wasn't him upset. That was him surprised and completely grossed out by the fact that I'm having sex."

"Right," Hal said, but he was still a stiff board in the circle of her arms.

She pressed a kiss against his chest. "It's no big deal. Warren isn't a gossip, but I'll talk to him later this afternoon and ask him to keep what he saw to himself, okay?"

Hal nodded, but he looked like he was only half-listening.

"Hal?" She cupped his face. "Tell me what you're thinking."

"I'm fine," he said. "It's all good, Savina. I need to grab my shirt. I'll be right back."

She didn't believe him, but she nodded and released him. He headed upstairs, and uneasiness making her a bit queasy, she grabbed the bread from the pantry and a mixing bowl from the cupboard.

When Hal returned, she tried to smile naturally at him. "How many pieces of French toast would you like?"

"Oh, actually, I have to go," Hal said. "I forgot I told

Solomon I would help him with something at the ranch this morning."

"Okay," she said, that unease growing steadily thicker. "Do you want to call me when you're finished, and we can have lunch together?"

"I'm not sure I'll be done by then, but yeah, I'll text as soon as I'm done." Hal headed toward the front door, and she trailed after him as he slipped into his jacket and grabbed his helmet.

"Hal?"

He stopped with his hand on the doorknob. After a moment, he turned and smiled at her, but his smile looked off.

"Are you okay?" she asked.

"I am," he said before leaning forward and pressing a quick kiss against her mouth. "I'll text you later."

He left, closing the door quietly behind him as a wave of cold apprehension settled over Savina.

CHAPTER 16

S avina slid out of her truck and walked toward the vet clinic. She was here to talk to Warren, but not seeing Hal's car or his bike in the parking lot was giving her already stressed out brain another thing to worry about. Hal had been acting strange and distant since he'd left Sunday morning, declining her invitation for dinner on Monday night and giving brief replies to her texts. It'd only been two days, but she couldn't sit around on her ass any longer. She would talk to Hal tonight, but, first, she wanted to speak to Warren and confirm that he and Hal weren't fighting or being weird with each other.

The reception area was empty and quiet and Laila smiled at her from behind the reception desk. "Hi, Savina. How are you?"

"I'm good. How come you're behind the desk today?" Savina asked.

Laila was the clinic manager and didn't typically handle reception.

"Oh, Brooklyn had a doctor's appointment, and Fatima

needed to leave early for her son's basketball game. Do you have an appointment this afternoon?" Laila scanned her computer screen. "I don't see you on the schedule."

"I don't have an appointment," Savina said. "I'm here to see Warren."

"Ah, well, he just finished his last appointment for the day, so he should be free. Head on to the back," Laila said.

"Thanks, Laila." Savina pushed through the swinging door that separated the rest of the clinic from the front foyer. A girl with bright green hair stood in the treatment area, drawing a clear liquid into a syringe.

Nathan stood at the treatment table, petting a large gray rabbit that sat docilely on the table. He glanced up. "Hi, Savina. How are you?"

"Good, thanks. How are you?"

"Good. If you're looking for Warren, he's in his office."

"Thanks." She headed toward Warren's office, knocking on the open door before stepping into the room. "Hey, Warren."

"Hey, Savina." He sat back in his chair as she shut the door behind her.

"Do you have a few minutes?"

"I do," he said. "You just missed Hal. He left early, said he had a headache and was feeling a little queasy."

"I'm here to see you," she said.

She sank into the chair opposite his desk as Warren said, "Is everything okay with you and Hal?"

"Why do you ask?" she said.

"He's been looking pretty miserable the last two days and even quieter than he usually is." Warren scrubbed at his jaw with one hand. "I apologized to him first thing

Monday morning, told him it just caught me off guard and that I should never have said what I did about you being his best friend's wife, but things still feel weird between us."

He leaned back in his chair. "I'm happy for the two of you, you know that, right? Hell, now that I've had time to think about it, I'm not even all that surprised. You two have been thick as thieves for years. When did you start dating?"

"We weren't dating," Savina said. "We were friends with benefits."

"Ah." Warren got that look on his face, the one that practically screamed, 'Abort Mission'.

Savina smiled, but it was a bit forced. "Don't worry, that's as much detail as I'm going to give you. I just stopped by to see if you and Hal had talked."

"Well, as I said, we did, but not sure if it's done much good. Has he been quiet with you?"

"I haven't seen him since Sunday. He left right after you did, and he's been avoiding me the last two days."

Warren frowned. "Should I talk to him again?"

"No, I'm heading to his place now to speak with him," Savina said.

Warren leaned forward, studying her intently. "You love him, don't you?"

She nodded. "I do. I've been in love with him for a while if I'm being honest. I just didn't have the guts to admit it to myself or him."

"Does he love you?" Warren asked bluntly.

"I think so. But I think he's struggling with guilt. At least, I think that's what's stopping him from admitting he loves me. I guess I'll find out tonight."

Warren smiled a little. "You do go after what you want without any fear. It's something I've always admired about you."

"Thanks, Warren." She stood and hugged him. "I'll let you know how it goes with Hal."

He returned her hug before smiling at her. "I hope Hal realizes what a lucky man he is."

HAL STARED INTO HIS MOSTLY EMPTY FRIDGE BEFORE closing the door and walking to the living room. He dropped onto the sofa, staring blankly at the ceiling. He'd told Warren he was leaving early because of a headache, and while it wasn't a lie, it was stretching the truth. His headache was mild and relieved by a couple of Advil, but the ache in his chest, that steady throb of pain with every fucking beat of his heart, wasn't so easily taken care of with a dose of ibuprofen.

He rubbed at his chest as if he could massage away the sorrow he'd felt since leaving Savina. It was a pointless gesture. He felt hollow and empty inside, nothing there but that constant beat of pain, and he had a horrible feeling that it would never diminish. He'd live the rest of his life with a continual ache for Savina.

Then go to her, you jackass. Stop moping around feeling sorry for yourself and go to her.

He couldn't, not after what happened on Sunday. It didn't matter that Warren had apologized to him. Hal couldn't get the look of shock on Warren's face out of his head, couldn't stop the "She's your best friend's wife" from playing on repeat in his brain.

The knock on his apartment door made him jerk with surprise. He stood, wondering if Mrs. Shelton from next door had gone on a baking kick again. She kept to herself but always brought over a loaf of banana bread whenever she got in the mood to bake.

He opened the door, his breath rushing out of his lungs when he saw Savina.

"Hello, Hal." She smiled at him, but he could see the nerves in it.

"Hi, Savina."

"Can I come in?"

"Uh, this isn't a good time, but -"

"I think it's a great time." She shouldered past him and hung her coat in the closet before marching into his tiny kitchen.

"Savina, what are you doing here?"

She opened the fridge and took out two beers, twisting the tops off of both before handing him one. "Drink, Hal."

"Why?"

"Because we need to talk." She drank half her beer with a few large swallows.

His stomach churning, Hal finished off half of his as well.

Savina nodded in satisfaction before walking to the living room. She stopped in front of the glass cabinet that housed his Wade figurines collection, studying them silently as he took another swallow of beer before leaving his bottle beside hers on the counter and joining her in the living room.

"You've been avoiding me," Savina said without looking up from the cabinet.

He thought about protesting before simply saying, "Yeah."

"Why?" She turned to face him, her beautiful face tense with anxiety. "Warren said he spoke with you yesterday morning and apologized to you for what he said."

"He did," Hal said.

"So, why have you been blowing me off?" she asked.

"It's been a busy couple of days and -"

"Don't, Hal." She cupped his face, staring up at him with frank earnestness. "Don't lie to me, okay? I'm a big girl, and I can take the truth. I want the truth, no matter how painful it is."

"I don't want to hurt you," he said.

"You're hurting me now."

She said it matter-of-factly, but he still flinched, and guilt hit him in a hard, hot rush. "Savina, I…"

"I'll tell you my truth," she said softly. "I love you, Hal. I don't want just a friends with benefits. I want a relationship with you because I am in love with you. I want you in my bed every night. I want to wake up to you every morning. I want you just as you are."

Pride washed over him at her bravery. He'd always admired her ability to say what she wanted or needed, and he wanted to shout his love for her to the fucking rooftops. But the guilt and regret were too heavy.

"Do you love me?" she asked.

He swallowed hard. He couldn't lie to her about this. "Yes."

Relief crossed her face, and she slid her arms around his waist. He pulled away, putting some distance between them as she stared at him in confusion. "What's wrong?"

"We can't be together, Savina."

"I'm not your best friend's wife anymore, Hal. I'm a widow and have been for three years. Alan is gone. I love him and will always love him, but he's dead and isn't coming back."

"I know," he said.

"Then why can't we be together?" she asked.

"It's my fault," he said.

"Alan dying is not your fault. He had cancer," Savina said in a soft and even tone. "You don't need to feel guilty about that."

"I don't... I mean... it's hard to explain," he said.

"Try," she said. "For me. For us."

He sucked in a deep breath, staring over her shoulder at the glass cabinet. "After Mary died, I had... well, I had some fucked up thoughts."

"That's a normal part of the grieving process," she said. "I had them too."

He barked harsh laughter. "Not like this. I would look at you and Alan, and Solomon and Heather, and all I could think was - why me? Why did I lose my wife, and Alan and Solomon got to keep theirs? I was so fucking jealous, Savina. I kept thinking how unfair it was that I was alone and miserable, and they weren't. For a while, the jealousy nearly ate me alive. What had Alan and Solomon done that was different from me? Why did they get to be happy with the women they loved while I put flowers every week on my dead wife's grave."

His eyes burned, and his throat turned so tight he could barely force the words out. "I never wished anything bad to happen. I swear I didn't, but the universe didn't care. It didn't need me to actually wish for anything. It just saw my jealousy and my anger, and it… it decided to even the score. So, it fucking killed Alan. You lost your husband because of my pettiness and my jealousy."

"Oh, honey." Savina's voice held compassion, not pity. She crowded close, and he didn't have the energy or will to push her away. He closed his eyes, his breath coming in harsh pants.

Her soft hands cupped his face again, and she wiped away the tears that slid down his cheeks. "Hal, look at me."

He didn't want to, but she squeezed his face gently and said it again. "Look at me, honey."

He opened his eyes, studying the same compassion in her gaze that radiated from her voice. "I want you to hear what I say to you right now. Really hear me. Okay?"

He nodded, and she pressed a soft kiss against his mouth. "Alan didn't die because you were jealous of him. He died because he got the shitty luck of stage four pancreatic cancer. That's it. That's why he died, honey. It had nothing to do with how you felt."

The lump in his throat made it nearly impossible to swallow. "I know I sound stupid and irrational."

"No, you don't," she said. "Do you think I haven't been jealous of Solomon and Heather? I have. Many, many times. Do you remember that woman you were dating when Alan died? Jennifer, I think?"

He nodded, and she said, "I was jealous of the two of you, even though I knew it wasn't that serious. Jealousy and feeling petty are all normal parts of the grieving process."

"I was a terrible friend," he said. "After Mary died, Alan and Solomon were there for me. They kept me going when I didn't think I could. I repaid them by being jealous and angry."

"Did you tell them how you felt?" she asked.

"No," he said. "I couldn't… I didn't want them to hate me or to know what an asshole I was."

She kissed him again. "You weren't being an asshole, and I know Alan. Even if you had told him, he would have understood, and wouldn't have judged, Hal. Neither would Solomon."

He stared at her. "You believe that, don't you?"

"Yes." She returned his gaze steadily. "Alan was your best friend for many years, but I was his wife, and I knew him better than anyone. He would have understood why you felt that way, honey."

The heavy weight he'd carried since Alan's death slowly dissipated until he felt light enough to fly. He took another deep breath as Savina pressed her hand against his heart. "He loved you, Hal. You were his best friend, and he told me so many times how thankful he was to have you in his life. Nothing could have destroyed his love for you. I promise."

She pulled him into her embrace, and he buried his face in her neck as he wrapped his arms around her and nearly crushed her body against his.

"I'm so sorry," he whispered. "I'm so fucking sorry, Savina."

"I know, honey." She rubbed his back with long, slow strokes. "It's okay."

They stood quietly for a few minutes before he finally leaned back to stare down at her. "I love you."

She smiled. "I love you too."

He brushed her hair back from his face. "I feel better."

"Good, I'm glad."

"I should probably start seeing my therapist again."

"Oh hell, yes," she said, making him laugh.

"I never wanted to hurt you," he said. "I shouldn't have avoided you, but I didn't know what the fuck to do. I didn't think we could be together."

"We can and we are," she said firmly. "You need to be prepared that people will gossip at first, but know that I don't give a flying fuck what anyone in this town thinks of us dating."

"I don't either," he said and was surprised and relieved to realize he meant it.

"Good." She kissed him hard before saying, "We have two options. We can start packing or -"

"Packing?" he said.

She grinned at him. "You're moving in with me. Is that a problem?"

"No, sweet Savina, it isn't," he said.

"Good. We can start packing, or we can go to your bedroom, where you spend the evening showing me how sorry you are for denying me your perfect body for the last two nights."

He grinned and pulled her close before nuzzling her neck. "I am ready to apologize repeatedly, my love."

She pressed a kiss against his chest. "You're a brilliant man, Hal McGinnis."

ABOUT THE AUTHOR

Elizabeth Kelly was born and raised in Ontario, Canada. She moved west as a teenager and now lives in Alberta with her husband and a menagerie of pets. She firmly believes that a person can survive solely on sushi and coffee, and only her husband's mad cooking skills prevents her from proving that theory.

For more information about Elizabeth, check out her website at

www.elizabethkelly.ca

facebook.com/EKellyBooks

twitter.com/ElizabethKBooks

instagram.com/elizabethkelly_author

amazon.com/Elizabeth-Kelly/e/B00EOHZ0MS

bookbub.com/authors/elizabeth-kelly

ALSO BY ELIZABETH KELLY

Tempted Series

Tempted

Twice Tempted

Forever Tempted

Breathless

Tempted Trilogy (Books 1-3)

Red Moon Series

Red Moon

Red Moon Rising

Dark Moon

Alpha Moon

Pale Moon

The Recruit Series

The Recruit (Book One)

The Recruit (Book Two)

The Recruit (Book Three)

The Recruit (Book Four)

The Recruit (Book Five)

The Recruit (Book Six)

The Shifters Series

Willow and the Wolf (Book One)

Ava and the Bear (Book Two)

Katarina and the Bird (Book Three)

Porter's Mate (Book Four)

Bria and the Tiger (Book Five)

Rosalie Undone (Book Six)

The Dragon's Mate (Book Seven)

Rise of the Jaguar (Book Eight)

The Draax Series

Reign (Book One)

Rule (Book Two)

Rebel (Book Three)

Surrender (Book Four)

Harmony Falls Series

Sweet Harmony (Book One)

Perfect Harmony (Book Two)

Forbidden Harmony (Book Three)

Redeeming Harmony (Book Four)

Absolute Harmony (Novella)

Seasoned Romance Series

Bet Your Heart on Me (Book One)

Take a Chance on Me (Book Two)

Individual Books